Purgatory, Inc.

M.E. Clayton

ISBN: 9780463193228

DEDICATION

For anyone who has ever had one of *those* bosses…LOL.

CONTENTS

ACKNOWLEDGMENTS

The first acknowledgment will always be my husband. There aren't enough words to express my gratitude for having this man in my life. There is a little bit of him in every hero that I dream up, and I can't thank God enough for bringing him into my life.

Second, there's my family; my daughter, my son, my grandchildren, my sister, and my mother. Family is everything, and I have one of the best. They are truly the best cheerleaders I could ever ask for, and I never forget just how truly blessed I am to have them in my life.

Then, of course, there's Kamala. This woman is not only my beta and idea guinea pig, but she's also one of my closest friends. She's been with me from the beginning of this journey, and we're going to ride this thing to the end. Kam's the encouragement that sparked it all, folks.

Finally, I'd like to thank everyone who's purchased, read, reviewed, shared, and supported me and my writing. Thank you so much for helping make this dream a reality and a happy, fun one at that. I cannot say thank you enough..

PROLOGUE

They were all fucking idiots; every last one of them.

How could I be expected to take this division to the next level when I was surrounded by incompetent fools? I mean, how hard was it to follow simple directions anyway?

Also, fuck the company's view on employee growth and development. If H.R. had the intelligence to hire competent people with brains to begin with, I wouldn't have to waste my time showing them how to tie their own fucking shoes.

I mean, fuck.

I had that twit, Beverly, talking about brainstorming work and home time management like I gave a fuck about her family or anyone else's. If they didn't want to put in the work hours, then they shouldn't be here. They could take their useless degrees and go flip burgers somewhere if they wanted to be home in time for dinner every night.

Besides, I was the boss. If I said that no one was going home until a project was completed, then no one was going the fuck home. Plus, it wasn't like they didn't get paid for their goddamn time. In my opinion, they got paid way more than what they were worth. Unfortunately-or I guess, fortunately for them-Melko paid well, whether you deserved it or not.

Plain and simple.

Then there was that stupid bitch, Callie, from H.R., and she was always trying to tell me that I needed to watch how I spoke to people. She was always telling me that I needed to understand that everyone responded to criticism differently, and that I needed to be sensitive to that. Well, fuck that shit. I wasn't here to hold my employees' dicks or pet their pussies. If they didn't have the backbone required to work for me, then they could quit. It wasn't like it was that hard to replace a fucking idiot anyway.

Goddamn it, this was *my* domain. I was the queen of this fucking castle, and if they didn't like it, they could leave. Or, better yet, I'd be more than happy to show them out the fucking door.

Plus, if it weren't enough that Callie and Beverly were stupid cunts, I ha
those two Hispanic bitches, Lucia and Carmen, thinking that they could hid
behind equal opportunity. I was all for equal opportunity if the peopl
benefitting from it weren't stupid. My team was made up of four women an
four men, and the only thing that made the women tolerable were the mer
Sure, Brent, Cody, Jeremiah, and Ryan were just as stupid and shortsighted a
the women, but at least they were nice to look at.

The more that I thought about my management team, the more that
needed to get out of here and grab a drink. If I stayed and gave anymor
thought to how stupid my team was, I'd burn the building down.

I shut my computer down, then gathered my stuff. I was pulling my jacke
off the garment rack when I heard a noise behind me. I whirled around, but
couldn't make out much with the darkness enveloping the office floor. It wa
past ten at night and there was no reason for anyone to be in the buildin
except for me. The cleaning crew didn't show up on this floor until afte
midnight.

I stepped out of the doorway from my office, and I had to squint my eye
to try to make out anything or anyone in the darkness. "Hello? Who's here?"

I jumped slightly when I saw a figure slowly emerging from the hallway t
my right. "I'm sorry. I didn't mean to scare you."

I narrowed my eyes. *What the fuck?* I hadn't authorized any overtime
Besides me, there was no reason for anyone to still be in the building afte
hours. I also sure as fuck didn't appreciate being startled. "What in the hell ar
you still doing here?"

"Uhm, I'm actually here to see you."

I folded my arms across my chest, my jacket wrapped around in betwee
my arms with my purse hanging off my shoulder. "And this couldn't wa
until the morning? You had to see me *now?*"

A careless shrug of the shoulder was all I got. "Morning wouldn't hav
worked for me."

Just like that, I saw red.

Like I gave a fuck what would work and what wouldn't work for anyon
other than me. *I* was the boss. "I don't have time for you right now. In cas
it's escaped your notice, it's past ten o'clock at night." I turned, and then ove
my shoulder, I added, "Don't make me remind you who calls the shor
around here. You make time for me, not the other way around."

I was on the floor before the confusion had ebbed, realizing what wa
happening. The pain radiating at my scalp when a hand had fisted in my hai
pulling and yanking me back, had stunned me. I was still slightly confused a
the wind was knocked out of my lungs as I was thrown to the floor.

However, realization and panic finally took root as I stared up into a pa
of eyes that were filled with so much hate that I was rendered immobile by it.

Spittle rained down on my face as words that I understood but couldn
quite comprehend were thrown at me. "You think you can bully people? Yo

think you can just treat people like shit and it's okay?" The words turned into screams. *"You think you can fuck with people's lives like you're God or something?!"*

I could have fought back, but shock at anyone daring to challenge me had really paralyzed me. The shock also had me ignoring the glint off the steel coming towards me. The plunges into my chest, neck, face…were they really happening?

Christ, they were.

I was being stabbed to death, but all I could think about was how dare anyone attack me because…*well, didn't they know who the fuck I was?*

CHAPTER 1
The Ninth Circle of Hell.

Callie ~

If you could name it, I had it.

I had the lavender-infused hand cream that was supposed to calm an soothe the spirit tucked safely away in my desk drawer. I had the essential oil infused bead bracelets that I religiously doused in lavender, peppermint, an lemongrass every evening adorning my delicate left wrist. My computer screensaver background was a relaxing dark grey with inspirational quote thrown haphazardly across the computer screen. I had even traded in m preferred choice of musical background tunes to play nothing but symphoni music; soothing and relaxing.

Once upon a time I, Callie Callows, used to just use regular hand crear that didn't boast of any relaxing properties. Once upon a time, bracelets ha been simple fashion accessories. Once upon a time, my compute screensavers had been quirky and fun. Once upon a time, the music playing a work had come from my iPod playlist that had everything from N.W.A. t Olivia Newton-John to George Strait.

Once upon a time, my office had been filled with pictures of my famil friends, and my favorite sports teams. Once upon a time, I'd had gifts tha had been given to me by my co-workers lining the bookshelves.

Once upon a time, my department had been recognized as the best in th western region. The back wall of my office could attest to that fact with all th plaques and certificates of achievements and recognition. My department use to have an open-door policy, and I'd had always made sure that my face wa recognizable throughout the building.

I was the Human Resources Manager for The Melko Corporation Northern California Division. Melko had offices located all throughout th country, and they specialized in medicinal science. Their Northern Californi office consisted of nothing but administrative work while their Central an Southern California Divisions were a combination of administrative an scientific. They had labs while the NCD had only one small on-site lab that was used for minor testing. All in all, Melko boasted of fourteen locations throughout the nation with Baltimore, Maryland housing its headquarters. The locations varied from science labs to administrative work to actual hospitals for experimental treatments.

Once upon a time, I'd been living the dream. I had graduated high school as valedictorian, then had gone on to graduate from Stanford with honors. I had interned for Melko during my junior and senior years in college, and I'd known, without a doubt, that Melko had been the place for me. I had worked my way up from being one of the many human resources assistants at Melko NCD to the Human Resources Manager position.

For five glorious years, I had worked my ass off to be a fair and approachable human resource manager. I had made sure to walk each of the fifteen floors that made up Melko NCD, and I had made sure that my face was familiar and friendly. I had wanted to shake the bad reputation that could often plague human resources.

Then The Ninth Circle of Hell had descended upon us all, and my life hasn't been the same since. Erasing all those once upon a times, I lived in Dante's Purgatory with my own personal chapter now, and that chapter was titled Hell in Deadly, Six-Inch, Red-Bottom Heels.

A year ago, the Division Manager for NCD had retired. He had put in a solid thirty years and had wanted to move on to the next phase of his life. Malcolm Hughes had been a wonderful and dedicated boss. He had managed to balance the good with the bad. He had been encouraging, yet firm. He had been strong, yet fair. Malcolm had just had it all. His retirement party had been attended by *everyone*. Even some team members from the central and southern divisions had made the trip up north to celebrate his retirement.

When Malcolm had announced his retirement, everyone had been on pins and needles over the flurry of rumors and speculation over who would be taking his place. I had put my money on Lucia Mendez, thinking that Lucia had been the best fit out of everyone qualified.

However, I'd been wrong.

So very wrong.

No, really.

So very, very, very wrong.

A week after Malcolm's official last day, Melko corporate employees had shown up with his replacement, Margot Livingston.

Margot. Fucking. Livingston.

Now, take the worse boss that you'd ever worked for, multiply them by a billion, and that was Margot.

An entire year later, the lavender scents, the calming beads, the prayers, the yoga, the aroma therapy, the masseuses, the pedicures, the self-help books…none of them had made any progress in restoring my once happy soul. Where I used to be a beacon of light for this division, I was now the enemy, and it was all because Margot Livingston was a grade-A bitch.

Margot was a horrible, awful, evil human being, and everyone was blamin me for not being able to end Margot's reign of terror, though I wanted to.

Oh, Lord, how I wanted to.

However, no one felt safe enough to put their grievances on paper an actually file a formal complaint against Margot. If I went after her without an documented proof, I knew that I'd be going after her alone, and I wasn't quit ready to risk my job for people that weren't going to back me up while defended their misery.

I'd seen it too many times.

You go and stand up for a person, but once that someone was confronte with the accusation, they would claim ignorance or try to play if off a nothing.

Still, I got it.

I really did.

No one wanted to be out of a job.

However, that still didn't change the facts. I'd fry, and I'd fry alone if went after Margot without any documented proof of harassment with me.

Nevertheless, that still didn't mean that I shouldn't be doing somethin about Margot. So, every time that Margot got out of hand, I'd have privat opportunity talks with her, and I'd been logging the employee contac discussions just to play it safe.

At least, it was Friday…well, Friday for most of us. Margot loved beatin everyone up during the weekends with email, after email, after email c directions and demands.

"You know headaches can't be proven, right? I mean, you can just *say* tha you have a headache without actually giving yourself one."

I ignored the voice that I knew as well as my own and continued to thum my head against the top of my oak desk. The steady beat of each thump ha actually turned out to be quite soothing. That was until one of Jeremia Jackson's (my work partner in crime) hands slipped in between my head an the desk, cushioning the thumps.

I sat upright since he interrupted my groove and narrowed my eyes at hin "You're fucking with my morning meeting calming ritual, Jay."

Jeremiah made himself at home by sitting on the corner of my desl "We've already been over this, babe. The only thing that's going to work is priest that's authorized in exorcisms," he replied consolingly.

I threw my head back against my chair and looked up at the ceiling. ' wonder where I can fit that into the department's budget."

"Employee morale," he suggested as if I were slow in the head for nc thinking of it sooner.

I brought my head back down and studied Jeremiah. "You know, if yo had any love for me whatsoever, you'd sacrifice your manhood and pipe her good one, so that she can chill the fuck out."

Jeremiah cringed. "I *do* love you, but you are out of your mind if you think that I'd ever go near that," he replied, shivering a bit. "I'd bet my paycheck that she's sporting a Venus Fly Trap, instead of a normal vagina."

I lifted my brows at that visual. "So, then what do you think about the rumors of her and Cody?"

Jeremiah shivered again. "I *don't* think about them. Hell, I don't *want* to think about them," he stressed. "Now quit being melodramatic, and let's get our asses up to the conference floor before she sends her flying monkeys after us." Jay's pep talk sucked, but I still complied.

I gathered my notebook, my notepad, and my pens. I had learned the hard way to always have an extra pen on hand in case the ink ran out of one of them. It would be so much easier to tape the meetings, but because Margot was so vicious, she had banned all recording devices from any of the meetings. We couldn't have proof of her harassment now, could we?

Jay and I had just entered the elevator to the top floor when Lucia Mendez and Brent Elliot scooted in behind us. Lucia was one of the senior department managers, and she nailed the mood as she hit the button for the fifteenth floor. "Christ, why do I always feel like I'm in a scene from The Hunger Games every time she calls a meeting?"

Brent and Jay were both senior project managers, so we were all very familiar. "Because it's survival of the fittest around that snake," Brent answered.

Jay shook his head. "It's pretty damn sad when we're all willing to throw each other under the bus just to redirect her attention, yet we're all okay with it," Jeremiah added. "Talk about cheering everyone on to save themselves."

Guilt felt like a sledgehammer to my chest. I was the manager of all employee relations, and I hadn't been able to make even one dent in Margot's professional personality. "I'm sorry, guys. I'm trying. I really am." Normally, I wouldn't speak so freely in front of people because my job title represented the upmost in confidentiality. However, Lucia, Brent, and Jeremiah were part of the cool-kids clique, and I trusted them.

Jay immediately went to my defense. "Nonsense, Callie. We are all very aware of what you're dealing with. You don't need to apologize to us."

Brent and Lucia mumbled their agreement, but I still felt wretched about making so little progress with that succubus that enjoyed draining our souls.

She was definitely the type to eat her young.

The elevator doors opened, and we all walked out onto the fifteenth floor that was occupied by Margot only. She shared her space with her assistant and her secretary, and you weren't allowed to bother her unless you'd been screened by *both* of them. It was like having to sit and wait to see The Great Wizard of Oz. Except that Margot wasn't great, and she was more of a witch than a wizard.

When Margot had first started working as the NCD man-or rather, woman in charge, she had spent a hefty amount on removing all the walls on her floor and changing them out from drywall to glass. She had wanted to b able to see everyone and anyone that was on her floor.

With that new development, I was able to see that the conference roor was already occupied by the rest of Margot's management team. There wa Beverly Sparks, a senior project manager, then Carmen Randall, the senic finance manager, then Cody Buckner, a senior department manager, and Rya Jones, a senior division manager.

Now, where Lucia, Brent, and Jeremiah were part of the cool kids clul Beverly, Carmen, and Cody were part of the ass kissers club. They were lik agreeable, malleable, little robots, never questioning Margot, believing that would land them on her good side.

Newsflash, fools: Margot *didn't have* a good side.

Then there was Ryan Jones. That man was a snake in the grass if ever saw one. It was almost as if Margot was his mentor, and he was trying t outshine her. He was conniving, manipulative, and just her cup of tea.

We all had non-official assigned seats in the conference room, and luckil I was flanked by Jeremiah and Lucia with Brent on the other side of Jeremial The rest of the table's order from Brent was Beverly, Carmen, Cody, the Ryan. The chair seated at the head of the table belonged to Margot.

As we took our seats, polite acknowledgments were made around th table. These weren't fun times, and I knew that everyone was working thei own self-made magic to keep their shit together for another meeting wit Cruella DeVille.

Now, while it sounded like I was being petty and immature to call he Cruella, I wasn't being either of those things.

Okay.

Maybe I was just a little bit, but if you ever saw her, you'd be shocked b the similarities.

Margot Livingston was already tall for a woman, spanning at about five foot-ten-inches, but that wasn't enough. She had to wear these six-inch heel that were more appropriate for a street corner than an administrative offic However, the extra height shrunk the men around her to a lowly level, makin her point. Margot was also so thin that her clavicle bones were supe prominent, and her hair was cut into a silvery-blonde bob that could onl come from an expensive hairdresser. Her eyes were a bright, cool, ice blu and they sat under brows that were severely arched. Her cheek bones wei sharp and angular, but I was pretty sure that came from being so thin. He lips were thin and wide, and they often disappeared when she'd get tha annoyed look on her face.

Plus, she was always dressed as if the CEO of Melko was going to surpris us at any time. Her outfits were classy and stylish, but they did nothing to hid her stick figure. Margot had no curves whatsoever. The woman needed to ea a sandwich or ten.

In comparison, I was rocking my body at a measly five-foot-four, and was a few sizes away from being Margot's size negative four. My clothes had tags that read extra-large or size fourteen. I wouldn't say that I was overweight, but I could stand to lose a few pounds. Most of my excess was gathered at my hips, ass, and thighs, but no matter how many goddamn squats I did, I couldn't shed the weight. All I had managed to do was firm that shit up, but it never shrunk. My boobs were a decent C-cup, but most people noticed my ass first.

I was also a Plain Jane. Whereas Margot's face always looked like a professional makeup crew had worked on her, I wore the minimal. I'd been blessed with my mother's complexion, so I didn't use face makeup. However, I usually played up my green eyes with dark kohl eyeliner and black mascara. Lipstick was for partying, so I never wore it at work. My face was heart-shaped with a pair of full lips, a slender nose, and fluidly arched brown brows that match the color of my hair, which I was pretty proud of. My hair was naturally wavy, and I kept it long and flowing when I wasn't at work. During work, it sat on the top of my head in a messy bun.

My eye makeup was also very waterproof. After trudging home, looking like a pitiful raccoon those first few months after Margot's arrival, I had started buying waterproof eye makeup.

Margot and I were complete opposites, and it amazed me how Margot put so much effort into her looks, but she made zero efforts to improve her personality or professionalism.

Once we were all seated, we had to wait another ten minutes before Margot made her entrance. That was another mindfuck that she enjoyed engaging in. We were to wait on her, not the other way around. So, if we weren't all seated by the time that the meeting started, then she wouldn't show, leaving us to just sit around. It had only taken us three meetings where someone had been late for all of us to create a Plan B in order to make the meetings in time. Now we always had someone on standby to step into our shoes if we're ever busy and Margot called an emergency meeting.

Finally, Margot entered the conference room, and one look at her face told me to strap on for a bumpy ride because she looked pissed.

Awesome.

CHAPTER 2
Who's the boss?

Callie ~

Margot's ass hadn't even hit the chair before she was already descending upo
us with the wrath of her god-*or demon*. Her icy eyes fell on each one of us a
she scanned the table. "Can anyone here tell me who the boss is of Melko
Northern California Division?"

Uh oh.

This was not good.

Poor Cody just couldn't help himself though. "Well, you are, Margot," h
answered as if he was going to win a prize for guessing the correct answer.

Margot leaned forward with her elbows on the conference table and he
hands clasped in front of her. She cocked her head as she looked over a
Cody. "You see, I thought so, too. However, I must not be," she replied. "
must not be because, if I was, then you people would do what the fuck
asked!"

Margot hadn't brought anything into the meeting with her, so we all had t
watch in horror as she grabbed Ryan's notepad-because he was closest to he
then flung it across the table, stopping to a skid right before it made contac
with Carmen.

Completely unacceptable.

"Margot, wh-" I started to say, but I should know better by now.

"Callie, this is not an H.R. issue, so your comments aren't needed at thi
moment," she spat. "This is about a member of my senior staff not being abl
to follow simple directions." Her gaze landed on Beverly. "Beverly, did I, c
did I not, tell you to send in the final adjustment costs before Monday?

If felt like all the air had been sucked out of the room. We were all white
knuckle bracing ourselves for the wrong answer Beverly was sure to give.

Because none of our answers were ever the right one.

Ever.

Beverly's eyes darted around, praying for some help, but she knew-*just li we all knew*-that she was on her own. Lucia hadn't been kidding when she'd said that these meetings were akin to The Hunger Games.

Sorry Beverly.

"We…well, uhm, it's only Friday morning and-"

Margot's scoff was loud enough to interrupt her. "So, do you always wait until the last minute to work on your assigned tasks?" She didn't wait for an answer. "No wonder you're always complaining that you're swamped. You obviously have no idea how to prioritize if you're putting tasks off until the last minute."

God bless the little simpleton because Cody decided to speak again. "Margot, I thought you said not to submit the final numbers until you verified the predictions for the May trials." Cody started flipping through his notebook. "Yeah, it's in my notes from Tuesday."

I cringed.

We *all* cringed.

Even Beverly cringed.

Margot shot her hate-filled eyes towards Cody. "Are you daring to suggest that I'm responsible for the fact that you can't take accurate notes, Cody?"

His big blue eyes rounded. "Uh…"

Then Brent spoke up, adding more fuel to Margot's crazy fire. "I have the same notations from Tuesday's meeting, Margot," he confirmed, trying to come to Cody's rescue, even though Cody didn't really deserve it, and Brent knew it was a lost cause.

If her head started spinning around via circa The Exorcist, I would not have been surprised. Her face took on the ugliest shade of red. "Well, if that was the direction I gave, then why didn't anyone come forward Wednesday or yesterday to touch base with me about May's trials? You guys wait until Friday to mention this when the deadline is Monday?" she seethed.

Did you see that?

Did you see how it was still not her fault?

I was certain that her manipulative abilities were actually a gift given to her at birth by Satan.

Also, could you hear the crickets? Because I sure the hell could.

Still, how did you tell Satan's Spawn that…hell no, no one thought to touch base with her because we spent most of our workdays avoiding the shit out of her. Well, with the exception of Ryan and Cody.

"Margot, I'll make sure you have everything you need by the end of the day and-"

"Oh, how generous of you, Beverly," Margot said, cutting her off again. "How kind of you to give me a deadline report on a Friday afternoon, ensuring that I'll have to spend my weekend working."

One. Two. Three. Four. Five. Six. Seven. Eight. Nine. Ten….

Okay, so much for counting to ten.

It took everything that I had to hold my tongue at her accusing Beverly of

making her have to work this weekend. Margot was *always* working on th
weekend. Our inboxes could attest to that.

Beverly plastered a smile on her face, then said, "You'll have it by nooi
Margot."

Margot gave her a sharp nod. "See that I do, Beverly."

The next hour was more of the same. Margot picked each of us apart-eve
Ryan-and we all sat around the table and took it. When she was finally don(
everyone got up to leave, but I stayed because no matter how unpleasant
was to interact with her, this was my job.

As soon as the conference room door shut behind Jeremiah, Margc
leaned back in her chair as she let out a deep breath. "What now, Callie?"

I peered at her from across the table. This was so pointless, but I had a jo
to do, and boy, did it need to be done when it came to this barracud:
"Margot, last time we talked, yo-"

She waved her hand in the air, swatting my comment away like it was a
annoying gnat. "Yeah, yeah, yeah, Callie. I remember. I need to work on ho\
I speak to people, blah, blah, blah."

Did I mention that Margot was a grownup at the age of fifty-eight?

Yeah, very mature.

I took a deep breath as I tried to steady my frayed nerves. "Margot, this i
about more than just how you address your team. Sometimes your approac
borders on illegal."

She rolled her eyes. "Illegal? Really, Callie? *Illegal?*"

One. Two. Three....

"Yes, Margot. *Illegal.* It is against the law to harass employees. It is als(
against the labor laws to create or encourage a hostile work enviro-"

"Demanding that employees do the work that they are getting paid to do i
creating a hostile work environment? That's preposterous, Callie."

"It's not what you say, Margot. It's ho-"

"Yeah, yeah, yeah…it's how I say it," she interrupted. "So, it's my fau
that I'm surrounded by a bunch of sensitive pussies?"

Sweet Baby Jesus.

"See? That's the kind of-"

"You know what, Callie? Maybe you should stop wasting my time witl
these little meetings of ours and work on thickening everyone else's skin
little bit," she threw at me as she leaned forward, resting her elbows on th
conference table. "People shouldn't be afraid to hear the truth every now an
again."

I chose to ignore that. "Margot, workplace harassment is a real th-"

She stood up, and once again, didn't let me finish. "I'm done here. I hav
shit to do, which does not include these touchy-feely meetings you insist o
subjecting me to."

"Margot-"

She lasted longer than I thought she would. Margot whirled aroun towards me, and with her palms flat on the table, she leaned into me. "Don't forget your place, Callie," she hissed. "Just because I humor you with these pointless little meetings does not mean you are special. If any of my employees have a problem with me, then they should have the balls to tell me, and not go tattling to Mom."

I stood up. While this wicked beast was my boss, I still wasn't going to let her talk to me like this in private. In public, around other employees, I had to respect the chain of command, and I did. However, privately was a different story. "I'm very aware that you have no respect for me, Margot. Still, the title which I hold in this company means something, and I won't tolerate being disrespected."

Margot straightened up to her artificial height, then crossed her arms over her chest. "Well, Callie, tell me what else you won't tolerate?"

One. Two. Three....

"Margot, I'm just asking for a little respect and consideration towards all the people who work hard for you," I uttered, feeling completely defeated.

Then she hit me where it hurt the most. "If I'm so horrible, Callie," she said, her voice like ice. "If I'm such a monster, then why hasn't there been any formal complaints filed against me?"

I sighed.

I sighed because we both knew that was her ace in the hole here. However, I still chose to stick with the truth. "Because everyone is scared of you, Margot."

Her eyes took on an evil glow, and she'd never looked so hideous. "As well they should be, Callie. You should probably take note of that." She ran her eyes down the length of me in disgust, then turned and walked out on me.

I hated that she had a reasonable, legal, valid point. As long as no one was willing to file a formal complaint against her, my hands were tied.

Fuck.

CHAPTER 3
Shanked in prison.

Callie ~

Christ, I was only twenty-eight-years-old, but I already felt like I was pushin
eighty.

Once upon a time, I enjoyed the sounds of music so loud that you coul
feel the bass in your chest. I enjoyed taking tequila shots and dancing th
night away. Plus, when the occasion called for it, I used to enjoy meeting
hot guy and letting him run his tongue all over my body.

However, these days, with all the stress and emotional beatings tha
Margot thrived on, I found that I was too tired to feel the beat, the tequil
was now used to drown out my sorrows, and I was too pathetic to attempt t
dance. Never mind the strange, sexy, hot guy with his bionic tongue. Luckil
the tequila was doing its job.

"Supposedly, she's *supposed* to retire in a couple of years," Brent said i
hopes of bringing some cheer to the table.

He failed.

"Christ and all His angels," Lucia mumbled. "Do you have any idea hov
much more of my soul she could crush in two years?"

We were all here, drinking away this jacked-up week. Normally, it was onl
me, Lucia, Brent, and Jeremiah in attendance at these little drunken pit
parties, but Margot had been on such a tear this week that Beverly, Carmer
and Cody had joined us.

I didn't mind much, but now this meant that I wasn't able to talk as free
as I usually did because I didn't necessarily trust Beverly, Carmen, or Cod
Plus, supposedly, Ryan was going to show up later. He'd had some stuff tha
he'd had to take care of before leaving the office for the day.

The bar manager had allowed us to push two tables together t
accommodate all seven of us, but we were still spread out enough that w
were all kind of having separate conversations. However, when the jukebo
had been turned off to make way for the DJ, we'd been able to hear eac

other better.

I had just finished taking a drink of my beer when Carmen shocked the shit out of me. "Why can't God just do us a solid and give her the plague or something?"

Brent laughed. "I'd settle for her just working somewhere else."

"But then she'd still be walking the earth, eating souls and destroying all hope for humanity," Beverly pointed out.

"So, then she has to die," Cody chimed in. "It's the only way to preserve future generations." We all started laughing. It was funny, but it wasn't. There was a little truth to what everyone was saying.

Margot was evil to the core, and I didn't understand it. By all accounts, she had a better life than most, so I couldn't understand how someone with so much ambition, success, and money could be such a horrible person.

"With our luck, she'll outlive us all and die peacefully in her sleep," Lucia grumbled.

"And you'd prefer it if she was hit by a bus instead?" Jay asked, laughing.

She waved away his suggestion. "Too messy and too fast," she retorted. "If anyone deserves to suffer, it's that she-devil."

Then Brent shocked us all by addressing the elephant that followed Cody around. "So, Cody, you're sitting here, stating the obvious that she clearly needs to die," he chimed in. "But what about the rumor that you're…helping her out every now and again?"

Cody rolled his eyes, but he was frank and honest. "I know what you guys think of me," he said, shrugging his shoulder. "While I might not be a part of the cool crowd, even I'm not stupid enough to put my dick anywhere near that level of evil."

I felt a pang of shame. "Cody-"

He flapped his hand at me, waving away whatever I'd been about to say. "It's cool, Callie. I'm not embarrassed to say that I'm doing the exact same thing that everyone else is doing, and that's just trying to survive. I might kiss her ass on the regular, but I'm not fucking it."

"So, if you could do her in, how would you do it?" Beverly asked.

Cody got a dreamy look in his eyes. "I'm not a fan of violence. I'd go for something simple like sending her on a cruise, then paying a member of the kitchen staff to push her over in the middle of the Atlantic or something clean and neat like that."

Everybody started chuckling, but I was very aware that I should end this kind of talk, considering the position that I held with the company. However, it'd been a hellish week and the tequila was flowing.

"So, how about you, Bev?" Cody asked.

"Torn apart by wild animals during a safari in Africa," she answered- *quickly, might I add.*

"Messy, but appropriate," Brent laughed.

Beverly looked over at Brent. "And how about you?"

"I'm particularly fond of Hannibal Lector," he chuckled. "I say throw he into a pit of wild boars."

I shuttered.

These people's hate ran deep.

"What about you, Jeremiah?" Brent asked.

"Her spine removed from her body by an evil wraith," he answered.

"Wow," I said. "That was so not the answer that I was expecting."

"It's a little farfetched, but totally cool, right?" he laughed.

"A *little* farfetched?" Lucia asked, taking a drink of her beer.

Jay smiled at her "So, what's your fantasy?"

Lucia arched a brow. "Suicide," she answered. "Stick her in a room where the television plays nothing but happy cartoons and spiritual uplifting programs until she does herself in." The entire table laughed. It was mean and we were being unfeeling, but the idea of Margot being surrounded b happiness until she hung herself was sadly hilarious.

"Okay, what about you, Carmen?" Lucia asked, passing her the baton.

"Honestly, I don't know if I'd want her to suffer or just rid the earth c her quickly and mercifully," she said. "Merciful for us, not her."

"So, you don't have a secret fantasy like her getting swallowed up by th copier or something like that?" Cody asked her.

"Maybe something like in that movie Ghost," she smiled. "You know where she dies, and then the demons rise up from Hell to carry her down t their master."

Jeremiah huffed. "I don't think even Hell wants that black-hearted bitch."

I felt Brent nudge my arm with his shoulder. "What about you, Callie How would you rid the world of Her Hideousness?"

I let out a laugh. "This conversation is so inappropriate."

Brent rolled his eyes. "Everything about that viper is inappropriate," h pointed out.

"Ugh, fine," I conceded. "If it were up to me, I'd like to see her go dow in spectacular flames before meeting an untimely demise."

"What kind of flames and what kind of demise?" Carmen asked.

"I don't know," I answered before elaborating. "Like, I don't know…like I'd like to see her get caught for embezzlement, insider trading, or somethin like that. Then, once her shame became public, she'd go to prison where she' get shanked for being a little bitch."

"Ooooooh," Cody cajoled. "Shanked in prison. I like it."

I shook my head. "We are so terrible," I admonished. "I'm going to g break the seal. I don't need to hear anymore." I laughed, then headed of towards the bar's restrooms.

I knew that we were all just letting off some steam, but it was bad Karm to wish that kind of thing upon another human being. Sure, Margot was th most horrible human being walking the planet, but making jokes about ho we'd like her to meet her maker was beneath us. We were better people tha that.

I also hadn't really needed to go to the restroom. I'd just needed a break from the conversation. Even though Carmen, Cody, and Beverly had joined in on the death jokes, I still didn't trust them. I didn't feel entirely comfortable with the way things had been going.

Once I made it to the restroom, I used my time to give myself a quick onceover. My eyes were a little red-courtesy of the tequila shots-but other than that, I didn't look too hammered. I used my fingers to clean up some of the eyeliner that was smudged underneath my eyes, and after washing my hands, I headed back towards the table.

I should have been watching where I was going, but because I'd been so lost in my head, thinking of an excuse to cut out early, I hadn't seen the six-foot-two-inch wall of muscle walking out of the men's restroom at the same time that I'd been exiting the women's restroom.

"Oomph," I exhaled, the wind literally being knocked out of my chest.

"Oh, shit," a masculine voice, deep and rugged, said as two firm hands latched onto my shoulders. "Are you alright?"

It took me a second to catch my breath, but that wasn't the reason that I couldn't speak. Nope. I looked up into what had to be the hottest, sexiest, most stunning guy in existence. That was also fucking saying something because, hello…Hayden Christensen, Henry Cavill, Armie Hammer…*duh.*

When I finally found my voice, the only thing that sounded was an incredulous, *"Holy shit."*

CHAPTER 4
I mean, are you real?

Theo ~

I looked down at the little sprite, and I couldn't help the smirk that crosse
my face.

She had caught my eye as soon as I had walked into Benji's earlier, but m
first item of business had been to grab a beer. It'd been a fucked-up week
and my partner, Darren, and I had needed to take the edge off. Benji's wa
known to be cop-friendly, and being a cop, it was hard to let loose unless yo
were surrounded by your own.

When I'd seen Sprite walking towards the restroom, Darren had laughe
at me when I had suddenly announced that I'd had to go take a piss. He ha
tipped his beer towards me and smiled.

Now, I wasn't a creep; I didn't stalk women, try to corner them, c
anything like that. However, this was the only way that I was going to be abl
to get up close and personal with her. She'd been sitting at a table with a fe\
men, and I wasn't about to approach her when one of them could easily b
her boyfriend or something.

It had also been pure luck that we had exited the restrooms at the sam
time. To me, that was a sign from The Good Lord above that Sprite wa
meant to go home with me tonight.

"Are you okay?" I asked again.

Her jade-colored eyes widened, and she started nodding. "Yeah. Ye
Mmmhmm."

I smiled because how could I not? "Are you sure?"

My eyes took this opportunity to rake her in. She had dark brown hair th\
was piled high on top of her head with wisps of it dancing around loosely. Sh
had perfectly arched brows, one higher than the other. Her emerald eyes wei
framed by long, thick, dark lashes that were currently accentuated by a littl
bit of eye makeup. She had a slender nose centered between two rosy cheek
and her lips looked like they belonged wrapped around a cock twenty

four/seven.

My cock, specifically.

At that thought, my dick started to twitch as my eyes went from her plump lips to her smooth, creamy, slender neck, then down to a pair of tits that were made for me to slide said cock through. She was wearing simple office attire; a white flowing blouse tucked into a snug-fitting black skirt that stopped mid-thigh. Her legs were bare, and her feet were covered by a pair of four-inch office-appropriate heels.

Her outfit was simple, but the way it looked on her made it anything but. She wasn't a skinny little thing, either. Nope. This girl had curves. She had tits o'plenty, a soft tummy, wide hips, and thick thighs, and my dick was taking painful notice. It had been taking notice all evening, but now, being so close to her, my dick was very aware of all her womanly curves.

Though my dick was getting hard at the idea of her curves, I thought women were beautiful in whatever shape or size they came in. I was a diehard fan of the female species. Still, there was something to be said for a woman's softness. Being a cop, I worked out whenever I could. It was imperative that I be in shape in my line of work. I had the shoulders, the pecs, the arms, the abs, and the legs. So, when I wanted to lay next to a woman, I wanted to revel in everything that made a woman different from a man, and that included all her hills and valleys. If I wanted muscle and bones, then I'd just feel myself up.

She was still staring up at me, all wide-eyed and open mouthed, and all I could think about was how I'd like to fill that opened mouth of hers. I reined in my train of thought and decided to introduce myself. "I'm Theo," I said, smiling.

She finally must have realized that she was staring because her eyes got wider, and she shook her head. "Oh, I'm sorry," she rushed out. "I'm…uhm, I'm Callie. Callie Callows."

"Callie," I repeated, tasting her name on my lips and liking it. "Well, it's nice to meet you, Callie Callows. I'm Theo Marsden." I ran my eyes down her body and back up one more time. "Are you sure that you're okay?"

"Oh, me? I'm fine," she huffed.

"Okay," I said before letting go of her shoulders. "If you're sure." I smiled again, and we stood there, just staring at one another for a few awkward seconds.

All of a sudden, she took me by complete surprise with her honesty. "Jesus Christ, you are one good-looking man," she practically panted. "I mean, are you real? Do you have any idea how good-looking you are? Like, are your parents otherworldly or something?"

I threw my head back and laughed. It was probably the first genuine laugh that I'd had all week. She must be drunk. Or unfiltered. Either way, she was a delight. "Uh, thanks," I finally remarked. "And to answer your questions, I *am* real. My parents are mortal. And I'm aware my looks are passable."

Callie's brows shot upward. *"Passable?"* She shook her head. "Dude."

Fuck it.

I stepped closer, crowding her until her back was up against the wall separating the restrooms from the view of the bar. I placed my hands flat on the wall next to her head, caging her in. Callie's palms pressed up against my chest when she couldn't back up any further. I wasn't sure if she was halting me or if she just wanted her hands on me.

God, please let her want her hands on me.

Her eyes kept flickering back and forth from my eyes to my lips, then back again, and I knew that she was feeling the same attraction that I was.

Thank fuck.

I leaned down until my lips were at the side of her face. "So, tell me, Callie Callows, do you have a boyfriend?" I asked.

Her fingers dug into my chest. "No," she whispered, then cleared her throat a little. "No."

I hadn't forgotten the crowd that she was with. "Are you here on a date?"

"No," she said again, this time, more clearly.

"Are you a virgin?"

She choked out a laugh. "No," she answered. "I haven't been one for few years now."

I pulled back, so that I could look into her face. I dipped my head, then took her bottom lip between my teeth, tugging on it until it escaped. "What's your social position on women who go home with men that they've just met?"

Her chest started heaving a bit. "Wh…what's yours?"

I almost sighed. She wanted to know if I would think that she was a slut if she went home with a man she just met. That was always a woman's worst fear and it sucked.

Women were sexual creatures, and they were created to be worshipped by man. They were created to accept us and submit to all the ways that we were meant to pleasure them. Unfortunately, they were always confined to what was socially acceptable. If women were allowed to explore their sexuality with no judgment-just as men were-they would rule the fucking world.

"How about this?" I asked, instead of answering her. "What's your social position on men who ask women to go home with them after they've just met?" I wanted her to know that if she looked bad for going home with me, then I'd look just as bad for asking her to. Contrary to popular belief, being a manwhore was nothing to brag about.

Callie raised her green eyes to meet my dark brown ones and said, "I… think that…" She had to clear her throat again. "I think that as long as no one's married or spoken for, it's okay."

Fuck, I wanted this woman something fierce. There was just something about her hesitant eagerness that made me want to explore her inhibitions.

"Just to be clear," I said, running my nose along her jaw, "you are not married, don't have a boyfriend, or are on a date, correct?"

Her breathing was labored. "No husband, no boyfriend, no date," she confirmed.

"Well, just for the record, I don't have a wife, girlfriend, or am on a date," I told her, pulling back, so that I could look into her face again. "However, I do have a friend at the bar who I'll have to let know I'm leaving."

Callie arched a brow. "So, you're leaving?" she teased.

I nodded. "I am," I teased back. "But not without *you.*"

"And what makes you think that I'm leaving with you?" she asked coyly because we both knew she was going to. Still, I was up for a little teasing.

"How about a little wager?" This time, both her eyebrows shot up. I leaned into her ear, then said, "If your pussy is as wet as I think it is, then you tell your friends goodbye and walk out of this bar with me. If it's dry, then I'll let you go back to your table, no harm, no foul." It was super forward and a dangerous gamble, but I was banking on her being just as attracted to me as I was to her.

Her eyes dilated, but her lids were hooded. "H…how will…how will you be able to…"

I smirked, and very slowly-*slow enough for her to stop me if she wanted to*-I took my right hand and lowered it until it rested on the exposed skin just above her knee. Maintaining eye contact the entire time, I gradually ran my hand up her inner thigh and under her skirt until I could feel the heat from her pussy.

My hand hovered near her center, waiting for her permission. Even if I weren't a cop, I would *never* make a move without the woman's permission. Callie let out a shaky breath, and the second that her feet stepped farther apart, I knew that I had her. My hand made the rest of the journey upward, and I slid a finger inside her cotton panties and through her pussy lips. Just like I'd been hoping, her slit was soaking wet. So wet that I could hear the slick noises my finger was making swimming in her cream.

Callie's hands shot out and grabbed onto my biceps. She let out a low mewl and started biting her bottom lip. Rubbing her folds wasn't enough. Another finger joined the first, and when I lodged them both up into her slick cunt, Callie threw her head back and let out the most delicious moan that I had ever heard.

I wanted to keep finger fucking her to orgasm, but I was still mindful of where we were. It wouldn't look good for me to get arrested for lewd and lascivious acts in public.

I'd never live it down.

Plus, every instinct that I possessed was telling me that this woman wasn't the type to give a show with a man she just met. The truth was that I was surprised that she was letting me do this much.

So, with much regret, I pulled my fingers from her pussy, and after putting them in my mouth and licking them clean, I said, "Now that I know what you taste like, baby, there's no way I'm letting you get out of going home with me." I kissed her temple. "Go tell your friends goodbye."

Callie let out a shuttered breath and said, "Okay."

CHAPTER 5
I almost sent out a search party.

Callie ~

Holy Mary, Mother of God.

I walked back to the table on wobbly legs, not believing that I had actually let a man-*that I just freakin' met*-finger me by the public restrooms.

What in the name of all that was slutty?

I mean…okay…the man was smokin' hot. Apparently, hot enough to short circuit my brain and turn me into an unconscionable whore.

Nonetheless, damn…

When I'd been stopped cold by his rock-hard body, I hadn't been expecting him to be all that he was. Looking up, I'd been knocked breathless and totally speechless by the beauty of the man.

Theo was around six-foot-two with dark brown hair that looked like it was meant to have a woman's fingers swimming through it at all times. He had matching dark brows that sat above a pair of chocolate-colored eyes that were surrounded by long, thick, full lashes that were wasted on a man. His nose was straight and perfectly centered on a face made up of prominent cheek bones, a pair of luscious lips, and a sharp jaw.

As for his body, I'd only gotten my hands on his chest and arms, but both times my hands had met hard, smooth, defined muscle. The man clearly made time for the gym, and it showed.

Plus, *Sweet Baby Jesus,* I'd already known that his hands were big and masculine when he had held my shoulders, holding me upward when I'd run into him. Still, when his fingers had found my heat, then smoothly slipped those two digits into my pussy, I could feel the stretch. The stretch from just *two* fingers.

Hell yeah, I was going home with him.

Only a fool would turn that perfect picture of maleness down. Plus, it'd been just sooooooooooooooooo damn long since I'd gotten laid.

I didn't look back as I made my way to the table. Theo had said that he

23

was going to settle up his tab and tell his friend he was leaving, so I figure that I'd use that opportunity to tell the others goodbye.

When I approached the table, Jeremiah was the first to comment on m absence. "Where the hell you been, Cal? I almost sent out a search party," h teased.

I was sure that Jeremiah could read all my sordid naughtiness on my fac but I tried to play it off the best that I could. "I'm fine as you can see," smiled. "Actually, I think I'm going to go ahead and leave-"

"Oh, c'mon, Callie," Lucia jumped in. "It's early as hell, and none of us ar anywhere near as drunk as we need to be in order to erase the nightmare tha this week has been."

"Yeah, Callie," Cody added. "Let's get fucking drunk."

Before I could come up with a casual excuse to leave, I felt heat envelo me from behind. Lucia, Beverly, and Carmen's eyes widened, and I knew was because Theo was standing behind me.

So much for a stealthy exit.

Jeremiah and Brent just smirked where Cody showed no expression at th newcomer.

"Uh, this is Theo," I introduced without bothering to look back at hin "Theo, these are my co-workers." I was too nervous to introduce them al plus I didn't think that Theo would remember their names anyway.

He gave them a blanket greeting. "Hello."

They all replied with a chorus of, "Hey, Theo."

Theo placed his hands on my shoulders before leaning into my ea "Ready to go?"

I nodded, then bit my lip when Brent, Jeremiah, and Lucia smirked at m Carmen's eyes narrowed a bit, and Cody was still oblivious. I walked over t where I'd been sitting, then grabbed my purse off the chair. I had paid as went, so I didn't have a tab.

"Okay, guys. I'll see you Monday," I mumbled awkwardly.

I glanced up at Theo, and he had a small smile lining his lips. He knew tha I was embarrassed. However, I wasn't embarrassed enough to put an end t this madness.

Theo Marsden was just too gorgeous to pass up.

When I made my way back to Theo, he gently placed his hand on th small of my back, then led us out of the bar, giving one final wave to th table. As soon as we were outside, he asked, "How did you get here tonight?'

I looked up into his perfect face, and I swear to God, it was hard t articulate simple sentences when his baby browns were focused on yo "I…uh, I had planned on getting drunk, so I took a cab."

He nodded. "My friend drove, so I guess we'll take a cab back to m place."

I started biting my lip again. Granted, it'd been a while since I'd gon home with a guy, and I was kind of rusty, but I thought the etiquette for one-night stand was to go to the nearest hotel. It seemed safer that way.

"If you prefer, I don't mind a hotel," I offered, in case he hadn't wanted to offend me. Of course, I couldn't even begin to imagine the impression that he already had of me after letting him do what he'd done by the restrooms, but something told me that Theo was a bit of a gentleman, even if everything else pointed to the contrary.

After flagging down a cab, Theo cocked his head at me as he stepped back onto the curb. "Does going back to my place make you feel uncomfortable?"

Hell no, it didn't.

It made me feel stupidly special.

"Doesn't it make *you* uncomfortable?" I returned.

He smiled. "Why would it?"

I could feel my eyes widen. I stepped back, then ran my arm up and down the length of him. "Because look at you," I exclaimed honestly. "Christ on a pogo stick, aren't you worried about crazy women knowing where you live?"

He chuckled as he opened the backdoor of the cab. "Are you saying that you're crazy?"

"Not particularly," I huffed. "But who knows what will happen once I see you naked. I might start doodling your name on my notebook at work."

Theo threw his head back and laughed. Once he calmed down, he looked back down at me, and his smile almost rendered me stupid. His left hand cupped my face and he said, "Well, I appreciate your concern and all, but for the record, this is a first." His voice dropped to a rugged whisper. "I want you in *my* bed, Callic. Not in some strange hotel room bed."

I couldn't stop the shiver that ran down my body.

Holy Bejesus.

He didn't say anything more as he guided me into the back of the cab. He gave the driver his address, and recognizing the street name, I almost gave a shout out to God because it was going to be a short drive to his house. There wouldn't be a whole lot of time for either of us to chicken out.

We sat on opposite sides of the cab, all buckled in and responsible like. However, I was secretly wishing that this was Las Vegas, and I could say to hell with safety and blow him in the back seat of this cab. Las Vegas cab drivers wouldn't blink an eye, but Sonoma cab drivers would.

The boring bastards.

Theo's voice snapped me out of my judgmental cab driver thoughts. "What are you thinking over there, sweet girl?"

Looking over at him, I decided on honesty. After all, I'd already let this man feel me up within minutes of meeting him, so it was kind of too late to worry about his impression of me. If he thought me a slut, so be it. I was never going to see him again after tonight, and the promise of seeing him naked was enough not to care if he thought that I had whorish ways or not.

"I was cursing the seatbelt safety laws all to hell," I answered, not concerned if the cab driver could hear me or not. "If California wasn't a clickit-or-ticket state, I'd have my head in your lap right now."

Theo closed his eyes, then let out the sexiest groan that I'd ever heard. When he opened them again, his gaze was full of so much heat that I could feel it reach me from across the cab. Apparently, he didn't care about the cab driver, either, because he asked, "Is that what you want? Is that how you want to start the night off tonight? Do you want to suck my dick, baby?"

I could feel a heavy pulse between my legs, and I just knew that I was leaking everywhere. His voice was like fire dancing across my skin, and Mary, Jesus, and Joseph, I wanted to hear him tell me to suck his dick just like that in exactly that voice-all night long.

My eyes glanced down at his crotch, and I could see a bulge forming. I looked back into his eyes, then said the most honest thing that I'd said in forever. "I want you to choke me with it."

It was surprisingly easy to be honest about your needs when you were never going to see the other person again. Shame didn't follow you home the next morning, so I had no problem being as filthy as I wanted to be.

Theo's hands fisted in his lap, and I knew that he was cursing the seatbelt laws all to hell, too. "Goddamn it, Callie," he growled.

I smiled at him impishly. "Are my plans interfering with your plans?"

The look that he gave me was scorching and in no way playful at all. "I still have the taste of your pussy on my tongue from licking my fingers clean earlier. So, yeah, your plans are interfering with mine because I had planned on spreading you wide open as soon as the front door shut behind us."

The cab driver coughed and cleared his throat, and I could feel my face burning red. Okay, so maybe I wasn't a wanton sex ninja after all, considering that his words could make me blush this badly. I ducked and turned my head to look out the window. I could hear Theo chuckle at my sudden turnabout, but I didn't mind. I knew that he wasn't laughing *at* me.

When the cab pulled up to Theo's address, I unbuckled my seatbelt as Theo reached for his wallet to pay for the ride. Theo got out first, and then walked around the cab to open my door and assist me onto the sidewalk. Together, he walked me up to his front door and all I could think was...*Oh. My. God.*

CHAPTER 6

Because I liked it rough.

Theo ~

I was thirty-one-years-old, and I was pretty sure that my dick had never been as hard as it was right at this moment, and that included my teenage years when I'd had walked around with a perpetual stiff one every day.

Callie was a confusing mix of shy and wanton, and it was driving me crazy. She'd been bold enough and turned on enough to let me finger fuck her at the bar, but she'd gotten shy when it'd been made obvious to her colleagues that she was going home with me. She'd been honest about wanting me to choke her with my cock, but she had blushed when the cab driver had overheard me talk about tasting her pussy. I was quite positive that she was going to drive me insane by the time the night was over.

I was fucking looking forward to it, too.

I unlocked the front door, then placing my hand on the small of her back, I guided Callie inside. I didn't bother with the lights since there was enough showing through the curtains from the outside streetlights, and she didn't mention them one way or the other.

Callie walked further into the living room as she took a curious look around, but she remained silent. I wondered if she was starting to get cold feet now that we were actually in my house.

I carefully removed my gun holster as she scanned the living room. I was a detective, so my holster was always covered by my shirt or jacket. I placed both the gun and waist holster in the top drawer of the table that decorated the entrance to my home.

Callie was too busy taking in my house, so she hadn't been paying me any attention, and I was glad that she hadn't been. People had varied reactions and opinions on guns, and I didn't want this night ruined if Callie happened to be anti-gun. I wanted a chance to tell her what I did for a living in conversation and not under the shock of seeing me with a gun.

She finished surveying what she could see from the living room, then

turned to finally face me. My steps faltered at the vision of her standing alon
in the center of my house. For a fleeting second, it looked like she belonge
there.

I found my footing again, and without a word, I stopped, then knelt dow
on my knees in front of her. Her eyes rounded, and she started panting, bu
she didn't break eye contact. Callie stared down at me as I ran my hands u
her legs, past her knees, underneath her skirt, and over her creamy thighs. H
breathing sounded labored, and her eyes clouded over in anticipation and lus
I hooked my fingers inside the waistband of her panties, then took my tim
pulling them down her legs.

Sweet Jesus, I could fucking *smell* her. She smelled sweet and inviting, an
I couldn't wait to spread her open and feast on her pussy.

When her panties met her ankles, Callie lifted one foot, and then the othe
When I removed her panties altogether, I flung them aside, not caring whei
they landed. Still holding her gaze in mine, I ran my hands back up her leg
until her professional pencil skirt was bunched up around her waist.

I finally looked away from her green gaze, and I was met with the site of
perfectly trimmed triangle of brown hair sitting above a pair of smooth, bar
pink pussy lips. It took everything that I had in me not to snake my tongu
out and taste her right then and there. I wanted to though.

Fuck, how I wanted to.

However, I wanted to eat her pussy with no obstructions, and in thi
position, I wouldn't be able to fit my face in between her legs like I wanted tc

I raised my eyes up the length of her body, and when they reached he
eyes, I said, "Step back, sit on the couch, then spread your legs open as wid
as they can go, Callie."

Her lips parted, and I could see the shyness trying to take over. Howeve
lucky for me, she quickly tamped that instinct down and complied. Takin
one step back, and holding her skirt up around her hips, she sat down befoi
opening her legs for whatever I wanted to do to her.

It was the most erotic sight that my eyes had ever seen.

I was still on my knees, but with just two moves forward, I was onl
inches away from her soaked pussy. I placed both my hands on the inside c
her thighs, keeping her legs from closing, ready to devour her. Still, I hadn
forgotten what she'd told me in the cab. I wanted to make sure that sh
understood that I hadn't forgotten about her wants and desires, even though
was putting mine before hers right now.

I looked up at her and said, "I'm going to eat this sweet pussy of youi
until you drown me in your cum, baby."

Callie whimpered, and even shrouded in darkness, I could see her fac
blushing, and I finally figured it out. Callie was a shy girl who *wanted* to b
aggressive. She just needed someone to encourage her dark desires.

"Then, after I'm done drinking from you, I'm going to give you what yo
want, baby. I'm going to push you to your knees, grab the back of your heac

then make you swallow every fucking inch of my cock." Callie moaned, and I swear to God, her pussy was so wet that I could actually *hear* it clenching.

I was going to blow my fucking load before I even got my dick inside her.

I was *that* desperate to bury my cock inside her, and she was *that* fucking hot; all curvy, soft, and smooth.

I couldn't wait any longer. My hands slid inward until my fingers were pulling her cunt lips apart. My tongue started at the opening of her entrance, then I swiped that motherfucker upward in one long, slow, firm stroke until it circled around her hard, pebbled, sensitive clit.

"Oh, God…" she moaned. "Theo…."

My name never sounded so perfect falling off someone's lips.

Also, from my lips to God's ears, I'd never licked a sweeter tasting pussy than Callie Callows'. I could spend all night down here and not feel cheated.

I started lapping her up like my favorite ice cream cone, and her hands drove into my hair, tightening with each stroke of my tongue. It wasn't long before she was feeling the frustration of being on the edge and not going over.

"Theo, please…"

I pulled back long enough to ask, "What, baby?" Callie whimpered, and it wasn't good enough. "You gotta say the words, sweet girl. Tell me what you want."

Her fists clenched in my hair, and she started moving her hips, trying to force an orgasm. "Please…" she mewled. "Please, make me cum."

Music to my fucking ears.

I slid two fingers into her leaking pussy, then curled them upward until I was rubbing that magical sweet spot. With my tongue on her clit and my fingers fucking her tight pussy, Callie exploded in a spectacular display of pure sluttiness. *"Theo…oh, God…"*

I kept finger fucking her until she rode out her orgasm, her body shaking with the sweet aftershocks of her explosion. There was no experience in the world better than making a woman cum. It didn't matter if she erupted by your fingers, tongue, or cock…it was a sight to behold any which way. Men who put their own pleasure before that of a woman's had no place on this earth.

I finally pulled my tongue from her clit and my fingers from her pussy, and I silently watched as Callie came down off her high. Her chest was heaving, her eyes were closed, and her spread thighs kept twitching in the aftermath of it all. My eyes took her in from head to toe, but they kept diverting back to her exposed cunt and glued to watching her cream flow from her body. My couch was going to be wet, but I didn't give one fuck. By the time tomorrow came, I hoped all my furniture was stained with her cum, sweat, and maybe blood, depending on how rough she liked it.

Because I liked it rough.

I didn't realize how long I'd been on my knees until I stood up, needing to shake the numbness from them. However, the discomfort was quickl forgotten when Callie's eyes followed my movements. She wasted no tim sliding to her knees in front of me, then going for my belt.

She was looking up at me and working at my zipper when her husky voic reached my ears. "Can you do me a favor and take off your shirt?"

Gladly.

I reached back, yanked my shirt over my head, then tossed it onto th floor. I looked back down at Callie, and the look in her eyes when she took i my naked torso was reward enough.

Her gaze was hungry and desperate, and I knew that she liked what sh saw. Never mind chasing bad guys-this moment, right here-the look in Callie eyes made all those hours at the gym worth it. She looked like she wanted t possess me.

I kept my hands at my sides and waited for her to push my boxer brie down and pull my dick out. I watched as she turned her gaze back to wh; she'd been doing, and I wanted to thump my goddamn chest when she let ou a swoosh of air at the sight of my hardened cock.

"Holy fucking shit," she whispered softly.

My right hand reached out, then cradled the back of her head, keeping h face lined up with my cock. "Remember what I said earlier?" She looked ur wide-eyed. "I said that I was going to make you swallow every fucking incl You remember that?"

Callie nodded. "Yeah," she whispered.

I fisted her hair in my hand, then shook her head a little. "That's nin inches of hard cock that I'm going to make you gag on, baby."

"Oh, God…" she moaned, turned on by my words, and I knew that I wa going to have fun with this woman. I loved to spew filthy shit when I fucke(and it looked like Callie liked to hear it. I was going to do everything that could to get her out of her comfort zone tonight.

"Suck my dick, baby."

Callie wasted no time. She took my dick in her hand, then bringing it t her lips, she swallowed me whole as far as she could. She was still missing few inches, but she was about to learn a quick lesson in that I always mean what I said and said what I meant.

CHAPTER 7
Make me.

Callie ~

I hadn't ever sucked a dick that was nine inches before. Hell, I fairly certain that I'd never crossed the six-inch mark. There was no way that I was going to be able to take his dick all the way down without looking like a sloppy, saliva-drooling, animated porn star.

Hell, maybe that's what he wanted.

Besides, after the eating out he had just given me, he deserved my best efforts. I was going to swallow as many of his inches as I possibly could. I started sucking his cock, running my tongue all over the head and underside ridge, working my way down as far as I could go.

"Fuck, yeah, baby," he groaned. "Suck my cock...that's it, swallow my dick..."

Incredibly, his words were making me drip. I'd never been with a guy who was as vocal as Theo, but I was quickly realizing how sexy his dirty words sounded and how turned on they made me. The few guys that I'd been with had been more of the grunting and moaning type. Now, don't get me wrong; I loved a good moan and grunt. However, there was something to be said for the dirty audio along with the dirty visual.

As I continued to run my tongue and lips over his length and width, it was evident that I wasn't going to be able to take all of him. Still, I didn't want to disappoint him. This god of a man had picked me out of everyone in the bar, and I was going to make sure that he didn't regret it. This was my one chance to be a sexual goddess, and I was not going to give up before the finish line.

I pulled my mouth off his dick, then throwing caution to the wind, I looked up at him and said, "Make me."

Theo growled, and it was the hottest thing to ever hit my ear drums.

My palms pressed flat up against his muscular thighs, and with an almost painful grip on my hair, Theo shoved his nine-inch cock down my throat. I gagged, and saliva started dripping, but I worked to control my breathing

through my nose. I also relaxed my throat muscles the best that I coul
because I wasn't looking to die tonight, no matter how hot Theo was. It wa
an endless ten seconds or so before he pulled back out.

Theo only waited a handful of seconds before he shoved his cock bac
down my throat, holding me still like he'd done the first time. As I felt th
head of his cock tap the back of my throat, all I could think about was ho\
lewd and pornographic I must look.

I also hoped that I wasn't going to suffocate to death. I did not need thi
to be my permanent forever story of how I died.

My eyes were watering with tears streaming down my face as I tried t
breathe and swallow Theo's nine inches of stiffness and live to tell about it.

He pulled out again, giving me a reprieve. I was still gulping for air whe
he used his hold on my hair to pull me to my feet. It was almost violent an
unfeeling, but his next words transformed those pockets of doubt int
unbridled craving.

He had my head pulled back with one hand as the other started ripping m
blouse down the middle. "I will never forget the sounds of you choking o
my cock for as long as I live, Callie."

Oh, God, he made dirty sound so good.

With my skirt still bunched up around my hips and my blouse torn dow
the middle, Theo ordered, "Show me those big ass tits of yours, baby."

I reached back and fumbled with the hooks until all three were free. M
bra fell open and down before catching on the rags of my blouse that wer
still hanging off my arms. Since I was a bit on the heavy side, I knew that m
breasts were full and heavy, but my skin still tingled with the praises fallin
from Theo's lips.

His right hand was still tangled in my hair, but his free hand came up t
knead, grab, and play with my chest. "I'm going to fuck these glorious tits c
yours before the sun comes up, Callie." *God, I could only hope so.* "I can't wait t
cover them with my cum." Theo angled my head until I was looking into h
deep, russet orbs. "I'm going to cum all over your fucking body until there
not even one inch of your flesh that I haven't kissed, tasted, fucked, c
dirtied."

"Yes," I whimpered.

Theo dipped his head, then took my left nipple into his mouth an
suckled with the perfect pressure of someone who was skilled at sucking tit
He sucked, nipped, and laved the hardened bud until it was reddened from h
attentions. "Fuck, what I want to do to these tits," he murmured.

Before I could respond, Theo was maneuvering us onto the couch, hir
sitting with his pants and boxers around his ankles, and me straddling hir
with my pussy over his rock-hard cock, my naked breasts up in his face.

He was going to make me ride him, and I didn't know whether to b
excited or scared. I was about to impale myself on a nine-inch cock, and I ha
no delusions that it wasn't going to hurt. I was not a porn star, no matter ho\

much I wanted to play at being one. My body was not conditioned to impale itself on nine inches of stiff dick.

Like…could he knock anything around in there?

Theo grabbed a hold of my hips and started pushing and pulling, making my pussy run along the hard, thick, hot length of his dick. I wanted to scream every time that the head of his cock brushed against my clit, but I just bit my lip instead.

I braced my hands on his shoulders, then looked down at his absolutely breathtaking face.

God, this man was fucking gorgeous.

There was no way around it. He should have models and heiresses sitting naked on his lap, not dumpy H.R. managers.

The words escaped me before I could control them. "God, you are so beautiful."

His eyes alit with a tender quality. He smiled as he replied, "Do my looks make everything else fade into the background? Because that's what your face and body do to me, Callie."

Theo leaned forward, then placed a kiss on my chest. He didn't go for my boob or start sucking my nipples. He just placed the sweetest kiss on my skin, and I could feel myself melting.

"Theo…" I whispered.

He looked back up into my eyes and said, "Your looks, your body, your smile, your fucking everything makes me want to do nothing but live with my dick inside your pussy for as long as I can, baby."

I was officially done for.

I had no idea if it was his looks, his words, the attraction, or my dry spell, but I was going to let this man do whatever he wanted to me, and I could only hope that it would be enough.

This was new territory for me, but the fact that I was never going to see him again encouraged a bravery in me that I usually didn't feel. As an H.R. manager, I often had to temper my reactions to situations and remain calm, reining in my natural instincts.

Theo being a one-time deal was the only thing that gave me the courage to leave all my inhibitions at the door. I could just be me and feel whatever it was that I was feeling without worrying about professionalism or popular opinion. I was never going to see him again after tonight.

Normally, I'd have some kind of reservation about what a man thought about me. Any other time, I never would have let a man finger me in public, worried that he would think that I was an easy slut. Still, something about Theo gave me freedom from my usually normal hang ups.

Maybe it was when he had asked me what I thought about a man who picked up women, expecting sex on the first night. It was like he knew that he could be judged, too, yet he was willing to take the chance for the opportunity to be with me.

That had made me feel desired.

Plus, trust me when I tell you, there's a difference between feeling loved, feeling wanted, and feeling desired. I knew that I wasn't ugly, but I was rather plain and a tad overweight. However, the heat in Theo's eyes, the dirty words falling from his lips, the urgency in his touch…it all made me feel desired. H made me feel like the perfect fantasy-*his* perfect female fantasy.

I decided to give myself over to the fantasy that he was making me feel like I was a part of. "I can't wait to feel you inside me," I moaned.

His eyes darkened, and his hold on my hips tightened. "If it wasn't such goddamn risk, I'd pull my phone out and record my cock splitting your tight pussy wide open, baby."

My entire core clenched at his wishful words. I found myself loving the idea, but he was right. These days, video was just too risky. To be hones pictures were risky, too.

"I'd record your lips wrapped around my cock, your pussy taking my dic deep, and I'd take a full-length picture of you on my bed covered in ropes o my cum from your face to your legs, then use it as my goddamn scree saver."

Jesus Christ, this man made me want to be a slut for him.

I didn't know what to say to all that. I'd never been good at dirty talk, an quite frankly, Theo just continued to leave me speechless. He stupefied me b his looks and rendered me mute with his words.

"Tell me what you're thinking, Callie," he murmured right before he too one of my nipples into his mouth again. I threw my head back and just felt. felt his thighs under my ass, his hands on my hips, his mouth on my breas and I realized rather quickly that a woman could lose herself in Theo Marsde so easily. "Callie?"

Right.

He had asked me a question.

It took me a second, but I was finally able to recall what he had asked "I'm thinking about how good you feel all around me." I was past the poir of trying to play coy and tease him.

He switched to the other nipple, but not before saying, "If you think tha I'm making you feel good now, just wait until I stuff you full of my dicl baby." Cocky or confident? I didn't know. Nor did I really care.

I rubbed myself up and back over his hardened length, and I had no doub that he was going to make me feel good with that thing. I'd wager that he wa going to make me feel goddamn fantastic with that thing that he was sportin between his legs. A nine-inch cock with damn near the thickness of cucumber was bound to make an impression. I just prayed that I could endur whatever he had planned. I wanted to be in this for the long haul.

Or at the very least, until the sun came up.

Theo released my nipple with a pop, then started kissing his way across m chest. When he got to my collarbone, he said, "I can't wait to mark your sof pale, unblemished skin." I let out a tiny yelp when he nipped at my flesh. "I can't wait to see my teeth marks on you."

"Theo…" I moaned because I couldn't wait to see them on me, either.

"Every man who looks at you is going to know that you've been claimed; that you're owned," he rattled off. Even though I knew that it was just lust talking, I liked the idea of his declarations.

God, I was so screwed.

CHAPTER 8
Do you want to stop?

Theo ~

I knew that Callie probably believed that I was just feeding her a line of bullshit with all that I was saying, but I wasn't. I didn't know what it was about her, but I meant the shit that I was saying. If I could find a way to live with my cock in her pussy, down her throat, or up her ass all day, every day, I would.

It had taken everything that I'd had in me not to blow my load when she had looked up at me, telling me to make her take my entire length earlier. She was like a wet dream come true.

I'd thought that I was going to have to rein in some of my urges, but Callie was proving to be game with the pace that I was setting, and that was fucking with my mind.

Fuck me running, when I had ripped her blouse open, and she had popped her bra off…I'd never seen a more magnificent pair of tits in all my life. I had every intention of sliding my cock in between those two beautiful mounds until I unleashed myself all over them.

I was also thankful that Callie was trying to hold her shyness at bay because I planned to fuck her like a dirty slut all night long. By the grace of God, by the time morning came, I should know what it feels like to cum down her throat, in her pussy, in her ass, on her tits, on her face, on her back, and just every-fucking-where else.

Just the thought had me done with foreplay. I grabbed Callie by her hips. "Ride my cock, baby," I commanded.

Callie balanced her weight on her knees, and then inched up, so that could line my dick up against her sweet opening. The second that I felt the head of my dick breach her opening, I knew that I was fucked. I was fucked because I *never* forgot the condom.

Since I'd lost my virginity to Sandra Bates at the tender age of fifteen, I'd always worn a condom, especially after working the vice beat before becoming a detective. I'd seen what unprotected sex could do to a person. It wasn't pretty, and it was a horrible way to live.

Now going back to me being fucked, I was fucked because I had the presence of mind to know that I should reach down in my pants pocket, get out my wallet, then pull out the condom that I *knew* was in there.

Still, I didn't.

I let Callie slide down over my cock, bare and unprotected, and I fucking saw stars.

Her pussy had the grip of a vise, and even with as wet as she was, Callie was still struggling to accept my size. Her slow ease down my cock was complete, utter, beautiful torture.

The unchivalrous, dirty, reckless part of my mind prayed that she didn't come to her senses and demand a condom. I was pretty sure that I'd burst into tears if she did.

However, while I was over here, praying that she lost all sense of responsibility, Callie was busy trying to take my cock, and it made me feel like a motherfucking god. "Theo…" she whimpered brokenly.

I used my hands to help guide her. "You can take it, baby," I soothed. *"Christ,* your pussy feels so fucking good, Callie."

That must have given her some encouragement because she placed her hands back on my shoulders, then slid her body all the way down until her ass was sitting on my thighs, and my cock was crammed all the way up her hot, snug, wet pussy.

Callie threw her head back. "Oh, God, Theo…it's too…much…" she cried. *"It's too big…"*

I didn't care how confident a man was; every guy loved to hear his woman cry out that she couldn't take his cock, and Callie's cries just made me want to rip her apart and ruin her for any other man.

"Do you want to stop?" I might want to shred her to pieces, but I wanted to do it with her unwavering consent. Every mark, every scratch, every bite, all of it was going to be done with her consent.

She shook her head, then looked back down at me. "No," she rasped. "I just need…need a minute." Have you ever seen a grown man cry? Well, I was pretty sure that would have been me had she said that she wanted me to stop.

Thank God, she hadn't.

Plus, call it a hunch, or just call me a bastard, but something told me that she might say she needed a minute to acclimate herself around me, but she really didn't want that minute.

"Too bad, baby," I grunted, and then without any warning, I took the hold that I had on her hips and started ramming my hardened cock up into her body.

"Theo…oh, God…oh, God…"

With her head thrown back again, eyes closed, and her tits bouncing in my face, I fucked her tight, pretty, little pussy for all I was worth. She didn't even

have a say in it anymore. My hands and arms were setting the pace, and I wa
bringing her down on my lap like she took nine inches of cock every day fo
breakfast.

I could feel every time that I bottomed out in her cervix and the feelin·
was unbelievable. I was going to cum so deep in her pussy that I was going t
flood her motherfucking *cervix*. I wasn't going to lie; I'd never been in
serious enough relationship where I hadn't always used condoms, but
couldn't wait to blow my stacks inside Callie and experience what that felt lik
for the first time ever.

Her fingers were digging into my shoulders, and though I couldn't hav
imagined it possible, my dick got harder when her nails broke the skin. Tha
slight sting of pain had me wanting to mark her as well.

So, I did.

Callie's head was thrown back, leaving her neck exposed in the mo·
deliciously vulnerable way. So, I leaned up, latched onto her neck, then bit th
holy fuck out of her. She screamed, and I sucked, still bringing her down o
my cock with enough force to leave bruises.

This was fucking.

Pure, unadulterated fucking.

"Oh, God," she cried. "I'm going to-"

Her voice cracked, but I knew what she was trying to say. Callie was abou
to cum and *thank fuck*. I wasn't sure how much longer I was going to be abl
to hold out. Being inside a tight, warm, wet pussy without a condom wa
unlike anything describable. The feeling was so sensational that unplanne
pregnancies made all the sense in the world to me right now. Because, *rig·
now,* if it were a choice between pulling out of Callie's tight warmth or stayin
buried inside her and getting her pregnant…well, we better start picking ou
baby names.

"That's it, Callie," I urged. "Cum on my cock, baby." She let out a gutte
cry. "Cum all over my cock, so I can cum in your pussy."

Finally, she did.

Callie screamed my name, and her cunt clamped down on my cock s
hard and so tight that I wasn't sure if I'd ever be free of her. The skin-on-ski
spasms pulled my orgasm out of me with so much force that I saw whit·
spots dance behind my eyes.

I unloaded everything that I had inside her, and she kept grinding agains
me, taking it.

It was the best orgasm of my fucking life.

The rush was so fresh and overpowering that my next immediate though
was how unreal her ass was going to feel, bare around my cock. Now tha
protection was irrelevant where Callie was concerned, I had every intention c
fucking her up the ass until I unloaded in there, too.

God, please let her be open to my cock in her ass.

Callie collapsed on top of me, and all you could hear was the aftermath c whimpers and the deep rush of our breathing. My hands stayed at her hips, rubbing and caressing, and her head rested on my right shoulder with her hands still latched onto my shoulders.

"Baby?"

"Hmm?"

I chuckled. It was probably a dick move to be so proud of myself but fuck it; I felt like I'd just conquered uncharted lands. "You okay?" I asked, running my hands up and down her back.

Her answer was muffled, but I could hear it anyway. "I might not be able to walk ever again, but I'm okay with that."

I laughed, and she hissed. My cock was softening, but it was still buried inside her. "Good to hear."

Callie leaned back, then looked down at me. Her face was open and honest with not a pretense in sight. "That was incredible," she mumbled.

I reached up, then ran my thumb across her bottom lip. "Yeah, it was."

She pressed down on my lap, keeping me seated inside her. "I've never had a dick this big inside me before."

I groaned. "Callie, baby…"

She shrugged a shoulder. "It's true."

I leaned up, then kissed her softly on the lips before it hit me. I fingered her, ate her pussy, shoved my dick in her mouth, and fucked her sore, but I still hadn't kissed her. That gave me a sense of discomfort that I didn't want to analyze.

I deepened the kiss, causing her to sigh as she opened up for me. We kissed for what felt like hours, and I would have happily gone on kissing her, but she started wiggling around.

I broke off the kiss, then helped her to stand. After a few minutes, when I was certain that she could stand on her own, I finished undressing her until she was standing before me completely naked, and my dick started to rise again.

I stood up, shedding myself of everything, and then I lifted her, carrying her to the bedroom. I laid her on the bed, then I covered her body with mine. Bracing my bodyweight on my arms, I looked down at her and gave her one last chance to bolt. "Callie, I meant what I said."

She sounded breathless with anxiousness. "When you said what?"

"Before the sun comes up, your entire body is going to be covered in my cum." Callie's hips rose of their own accord, and she let out a low whimper. "If you don't want that, you have to tell me now," I demanded.

I could see the conviction in her eyes as she said, "I want it all, Theo. Everything you have to give."

CHAPTER 9
Mother. Fuck. Me.

Callie ~

My eyes slowly started to work, and I was disoriented for a few second
before I went to roll over, then the aches and pains radiating throughout m
body reminded me of where I was.

I was in Theo's bed, and it was the horrible morning-after.

I let out a deep breath and did my best to relax back onto the bed, but
was hard.

My body fucking hurt.

From head to freakin' toe, my body ached like I'd been hit by a goddam
bus.

Theo wasn't touching me, but I could feel his body heat from his side o
the bed, and all I could hope for was that I'd be able to get out of her
without him waking up.

It wasn't that I was embarrassed about last night; on the contrary, la
night had been the best sexual experience of my life. Hell, the odds were th
it was going to be the best sexual experience of my life *ever*. No matter where
went from here, or who I moved on with, Theo Marsden was going to be
hard act to follow. During the night, he had teased that he was going to rui
me for all other men, and I was pretty sure that the sonofabitch might hav
made good on that promise.

I closed my eyes as random snippets of last night danced across m
memory. I had let Theo use me like we'd known and trusted each other fc
years. I had let him inside my body without any protection or thought c
protection. I had exposed my darkest and dirtiest secrets, and the more I ha
given, the more he had taken.

I wished that I could say that I felt some sort of shame or remorse thi
morning, but I didn't. I did not regret one single thing that Theo had done t
me last night, or anything that I'd done to him for that matter.

However, one thing was for certain; if he hadn't thought that I was complete slut when I had let him finger me at the bar last night, he had to think that I was one now.

I ran my hands over my face, recalling how I had even let him inside my ass last night.

What kind of woman let a man she just *met stick it in her goddamn ass?*

Still, that's how high I'd been off his touches, his kisses, and that freakin' nine-inch cock.

I'd never done anal before because…well, once upon a time, anal had been for that someone special. That one person who you loved and trusted. That one person who would appreciate and understand how much you trusted them with something like that.

Well, I guess, now, apparently, anal was reserved for sex gods with nine-inch cocks.

Sighing for the love of everything sexual, knowing what I knew now, a nine-inch cock was *not* the way to break in anal play. The only reason that Theo hadn't torn me to shreds was because my body had been so limp and exhausted from the endless number of orgasms that he had rung out of me that my body had readily opened up for him. Now, that wasn't to say it hadn't hurt like a bitch, because it had. Still, once he got going…well, have you ever had an anal orgasm?

Mother. Hubbard.

Thank God it was only Saturday because I was going to need today and tomorrow to recuperate before being able to walk without a limp at work on Monday.

I held my breath, then slowly rolled out of the bed, hoping against all hope that Theo didn't wake up. I didn't sit up and throw my legs over like a normal person. No. I relaxed my body the best that I could, then rolled my entire frame, letting my legs roll off first. Bending at the knees, then allowing my upper body to follow suit until I was on the floor next to the bed, my eyes peeked up over the mattress, checking to see if Theo had awoken.

Thank you, Jesus, he hadn't.

I crawled-yes, crawled-towards the bedroom door, then made my escape out to the living room. No, it was not one of my finest moments, but I didn't care. My crawling escape made sense for two reasons; the first being that I didn't want to wake Theo. The second being that my body was so sore that I was pretty sure I'd be screaming in agony if I tried to actually walk.

The first thing that I was going to do when I got home was take a scalding hot bubble bath and soak everything from the waist down.

Goddamn anal sex.

Luckily, all my clothes-or what was left of them-were still piled where they'd been discarded last night. My shirt was a tattered, ruined, useless mess, so I grabbed Theo's shirt and threw it on. He might be pissed, but I was never going to see him again, so who cared?

I sat on my very sore ass, then pulled my skirt up over my legs until I finally had to stand to drag it up to my waist. Every movement was

uncomfortable, but it wasn't as painful as I had anticipated. I grabbed m
purse and heels, deciding to wait to put them on once I was outside, then lik
a quiet thief in the night-or morning as was this case-I cracked the front doo
open as quietly as humanly possible.

After shutting it behind me with ninja precision, I slipped on my heel
then walked down the walkway to the sidewalk. It wasn't until I was at th
end of the block that I pulled out my phone and used my Uber app.

I made sure to walk well into the next block over before giving an addres
I didn't want Theo waking up and still being able to catch me. However,
was still very early, and considering that we hadn't passed out until after fou
this morning, I didn't think that he'd be getting up any time soon anyway.
was still only eight on a Saturday morning.

The Uber car pulled up, and I got in without giving any consideration t
how I must look. I hadn't even gone to the bathroom to pee or look myse
over. I just ran-okay, *crawled* out of Theo's house like a true morning-afte
victim.

The driver was a woman-*thank God*-and after I gave her my address, sh
seemed to know the score. "Fun night?"

I laughed. "The best."

"But…"

I let out a sigh. "But it was meant to be just a one-night stand," I admitte
I didn't know this woman, but like Theo, I was never going to see her agair
so there was no harm in sharing.

She navigated the streets and conversed like a pro. "Ah, those are the be
kind of nights."

I smiled. "How bad do I look?"

She laughed back. "Not as bad as I've seen in my time, but obviou
enough," she answered.

The rest of the ride was made in silence, and once she pulled up in fror
of my condominium building, I slipped her an additional tip, thanked he
then dragged myself into the building and towards the elevator, then to th
sixth floor.

I almost wept when I saw my front door.

I unlocked the door, shut and locked it behind me, then headed straigl
for the bathroom, discarding my clothes-well, and Theo's shirt-as I went.

The mirror reflected sure fire signs of a morning-after participant, but
couldn't summon up the energy to care. It was done and over with. I had a
entire night of erotic memories, and a million things had been checked off m
sexual bucket list.

I grabbed the bubble bath and bath salts, then started filling the tub. Whe
I couldn't hold my bladder any longer, I went over to the toilet to pee as th
bathtub filled.

It was the most agonizing, horrifying, painful experience of my life.

"Motherfucker!"

My entire nether regions felt like they were on goddamn fire.

I had never felt anything like it in all my life, and mind you, I was attesting to that even after having a nine-inch cock in my ass last night.

"Oh, God…oh, God…oh, God…" I chanted and whimpered.

When the stream of volcanic fire finally dwindled, I pulled a couple of sheets of toilet paper, then ever so gently, I dabbed myself clean.

I flushed the toilet, then went straight for the tub. The water was hotter than I usually preferred, but that burn was a much better option than the burn between my legs.

Mother. Fuck. Me.

I eased into the tub, then turned off the water when I was covered up to my neck in bubbles. It took a few minutes for my body to start to relax, but soon, I was able to feel the tension in my muscles ease.

I dropped my head back, then closed my eyes, wondering why all those romance movies and novels lied. They always made it seem like being fucked all night long was a dreamy fantasy, but they left out the reality of the aftermath.

They neglected to inform you of a few things. Like, if you truly did get lucky enough to get screwed all night long, your body from the waist down was going to feel like it's on fire the next morning.

It was misleading as hell.

Not to mention the obvious that I was trying to ignore.

When I had glanced at myself in the mirror, my eyes couldn't help but to take in all the hickeys, bruises, and bite marks that decorated my body.

Theo had made random comments last night about being his and making sure that everyone knew it. At the time, I had just chalked it up to heated sex talk, but taking in my body from neck to thighs, he must have meant it because I looked like I'd been attacked.

I soaked in the tub until the water turned cold, and then I got out and took a proper shower before falling dead on my bed where I planned to remain for the rest of the weekend.

CHAPTER 10
Thank God for scarves.

Callie ~

My mind kept racing towards the clock, and I didn't know why. I just had a
ugly feeling about today. You know, that sinking feeling in the pit of you
stomach? Yeah, I'd been feeling that all morning.

Now, you would think that after getting the holy hell fucked out of me o
Friday night and resting all of Saturday and Sunday that I'd be rested an
relaxed for a Monday morning, but nope.

I wasn't relaxed in the slightest.

Call it intuition or straight up paranoia, but I had a feeling that Margot wa
up to something, and it was going to be the beginning of another week fron
hell.

Granted, every week felt like a week from hell-minus the weeks that sh
was on vacation-but today felt exceptionally dreadful.

My eyes were studying the clock again when Jeremiah's voice hit my ear:
"I've tried that already," he said, walking into my office. "That whole trying t
stop time or reverse the clock to avoid the morning meeting, I've tried that. I
doesn't work."

I smiled at my friend. "What does work, then?"

He sighed as he planted his ass on the corner of my desk, per usual. "I'n
sad to say nothing as of yet. However, I haven't given up looking for
miracle."

I eyed him, then decided to get serious. "I have a bad feeling, Jay."

He arched a perfectly groom brow. "Worse than the usual?"

I nodded. "Yep."

He started biting on his bottom lip, and I briefly wondered how it was tha
he could be so handsome, yet I'd never fallen into the feeling of bein
attracted to him.

Jeremiah was six-foot of pure male, and he was the epitome of tall, darl
and handsome. He had the most intelligent brown eyes that you ever saw, an

his complexion was a perfect blend of cocoa. He worked out and always kept his grooming up. It was such a shame that I wasn't attracted to him. I absolutely loved him to death, and he would have been an awesome boyfriend.

Jay threw me a wink, and then smirked at me. "You sure it has nothing to do with the new friend you made Friday night?" He laughed as he pretended to go for my scarf.

I jerked back and stink-eyed him. "Shut your face, Jay."

When I'd finally found myself back among the land of the living on Sunday, I'd found that Theo's territorial marks had been worse than I'd thought. They ran deep, dark, and damn near permanent. Every mark that he'd left on my body was just as prominent as it had been on the night that he'd made it.

I had done my best to fade them out with makeup, but some were uncoverable.

Thank God for scarves.

Jeremiah laughed. "Oh, c'mon Cee Cee." He only called me Cee Cee when we were being up-close and personal. "I'm not judging," he said. "You know that I'd never judge you for something like that."

I let out a deep sigh. "I know you wouldn't," I conceded. "And the anxious feeling in my soul has nothing to do with Friday night or Theo. I promise."

He cocked his head at me in thought. After a few seconds, he said, "Okay…well, it could be something or it could be nothing. Still, the fact is that we won't know if we don't get our asses upstairs to the meeting."

"I know," I mumbled.

"Look, Callie, what can she do that's worse than what she already does on a daily basis?"

I gave him a half grin. "Well, I guess when you put it that way…" He laughed, then we headed towards our morning management meeting together.

When we got there, everyone was already seated, and for a brief moment, I worried that someone might comment on me leaving the bar with Theo on Friday. However, it was just strained smiles all around as me and Jay took our seats.

It was ten anxiety-filled minutes later when Margot made her appearance. She sat down in her seat, and that sinking feeling in the pit of my stomach finally had validation.

"Callie, as of this morning, I am suspending all employee appreciation programs, and you'll need to send out a division-wide personnel email, informing everyone of this change," she said with just a touch of snark behind her words.

"Wh…What?"

What. In. The. Fresh. Hell?

She arched a brow. "You heard me."

"But…but *why?*"

"It's a waste of time and money," she simply answered.

"A waste of time and money," I echoed. "How can that be when we hav a budget for employee engagement and activities?" I was probably cutting m own throat right now, calling her on her bullshit, but shock was making m careless.

She laid her arms over one another on the table as she leaned forwarc "Monies that I've decided would be better allocated towards other elements."

This fucking bitch.

Margot was setting me up to be hated by all the employees. Sending a email out like that would give off the impression that the employees weren valued or appreciated.

"Margot-"

"I'm done with this topic, Callie," she said, cutting me off. "Send out th email and be done with it."

I was seething. I knew that she was retaliating against me for standing u to her on Friday. Or, at least, I *had* thought it was retaliation until she move on over to Brent.

"Brent, the presentation for the revamping of the biometrics program shit, and you'll need to start over."

What in the ever-lovin' hell?

I could see Brent's hands shaking with carefully controlled rage. "Margo that presentation took three weeks to finalize," he pointed out. "You gav your approval on it last Wednesday for final presentation."

"Yes, I did," she replied coolly. "But upon further consideration, I'v realized that it's subpar at best, and it needs some work."

Before Brent could jump across the conference table and strangle he Margot directed her next dose of venom at Beverly. "Also, with these ne\ developments, I'm going to have to rescind my approval for your vacatior Beverly."

Beverly's eyes widened. "But…but, Margot," she stuttered, "I alread bought my tickets for New York. I've booked everything. My vacation is onl two weeks away."

Margot straightened her back as she eyed Beverly. "Well, then it's a goo thing that you're paid so well, Beverly. The loss of your reservations isn going to make you homeless, is it?"

"Well, no…but-" Margot tossed her hand in the air, effectively dismissin whatever else Beverly intended to say.

What in the hell was going on?

Continuing on with her reign of terror, she said, "Cody, Lucia, you department equipment improvement requests are denied, so you're just goin to have to both find a way to make the current equipment work."

"Margot," Lucia balked, "that equipment is unlawfully outdated to run th trials required by the medical board. Every division of Melko is budgeted fc state-of-the-art replacement."

"Well, NCD is more geared towards administrative issues, and that's what we're going to focus on," she retorted while Cody remained quiet.

"Carmen, after this meeting is concluded, I need you to follow me to my office, so that we can go over the new allotment of funds and project costs," she directed before moving on to Jeremiah next.

"Margot-"

"Shut up, Callie," she snapped. "Jeremiah, it is up to you to follow up and personally handle any issues that Lucia and Cody claim are causing problems with the so-called faulty equipment."

I honestly wondered if Jeremiah was going to have a job after this. "There's nothing *so-called* about it, Margot," he replied. "I've personally already seen some of the inaccurate findings that have resulted from-"

"I'm not asking you about what you've witnessed so far, Jeremiah," she interrupted. "I am *telling you* that I expect a full detailed account of Lucia and Cody's claims moving forward."

Before Jeremiah could tell Margot to go fuck herself, she turned away from him, then went on for another forty minutes of non-stop demands and unrealistic expectations. By the time that she adjourned the meeting, my blood was boiling, and I knew that I wasn't the only one itching to throw Margot out the window.

She dismissed us all, but before she cleared the doorway, she looked back at us and said, "And if there is anyone here who is not up to the challenges presented today, let me know and I'll replace you with someone who is up to the task." Margot's words were met with stony silence, and with a smirk that I wanted to slap off her smug face, she added, "And please do me the courtesy of waiting until you're off the clock to cry and bemoan about how life is so unfair."

Arching a brow, she turned her back on us, and then walked out.

CHAPTER 11

It was utterly ridiculous.

Callie ~

I was pacing the floor of my office when the door was thrown open an
Brent, Jeremiah, and Lucia stormed in.

I stopped, then rested my ass on the edge of my desk as Brent shut m
office door.

Five. Four. Three…

"That fucking bitch," Brent seethed.

"Seriously," Lucia joined in. "And, of course, Ryan was spared as always."

Jeremiah was quiet, but I knew that it was because he was stewing and nc
because he didn't agree with Brent and Lucia.

"I can't believe that no-good cunt cancelled Beverly's vacation," Brer
went on. "What kind of…of…Jesus, I can't even think up a word bad enoug
to describe her."

"Yeah," Lucia snorted. "Calling her a cunt is considered a compliment."

I winced at their use of that word, but I couldn't really fault them. I looke
over at Jeremiah. "Jay?"

He just shook his head, staring at his feet. "I just don't fucking get it," h
muttered. He looked up over at me. "What the fuck is *wrong* with that bitch?"

I sighed. It sucked that I was the only person that they could come to fc
this, and I was pretty much powerless to help them. "I don't know, Jay."

"God, I just want to strangle that stupid…stupid…whatever the fuck sh
is," Brent hissed.

I sat down in my chair, feeling utterly and totally worthless. I looked uɪ
and Jeremiah was perched on the edge of my desk. Brent was standing in th
middle of the room, and Lucia was seated on one of the open armchairs.

As I scanned their faces, I said, "Look, guys, I'm really, really sorry. I wis
there was something I could do. However, without any formal complaint
about her behavior, my hands are tied."

"That's such bullshit, Callie," Brent snapped.

"Oh, hey," Jeremiah piped up, ready to defend me.

Brent shook his head. "What I mean is, even if we did file a formal complaint on paper, it'll just look like we're a bunch of cry baby fucks that are complaining about having to do our jobs," he clarified.

"What do you mean?"

"If I filed a complaint right now, what would I even put on it? That Margot approved a presentation, but then changed her mind and instructed me to redo it? That doesn't look like harassment," Brent argued. "That just looks like the boss telling an employee to improve upon a presentation."

I felt Lucia's sigh like it was my own. "He's right. On paper, it'll just look like we're bitching about having to do our jobs. Corporate H.R. has to actually *witness* her behavior."

"Or see a recording of it," Jeremiah added.

My brows shot up to my hairline. "Are you suggesting we secretly record the meetings?"

"How else are we going to prove what a fucking tyrant she is?" Jeremiah asked.

Before I could answer him, there was a knock on the door. "Come in," I called out. Beverly walked in, and it was evident that she'd been crying. I stood up as I regarded her. "Would you like to speak in priva-"

She shook her head as Brent closed the door behind her. "No, it's okay," she muttered.

"I'm so sorry about your vacation, Beverly," I said sincerely, but ineffectively.

Beverly straightened her shoulders, and I could hear the conviction in her voice. "I want you to see if she can cancel my vacation legally or…by company policy," she said. "If nothing else, I want to be reimbursed for my expenses, Callie."

I nodded in approval, not that Beverly needed my approval or even wanted it. Still, I was proud of her. I sat back down, then pulled up the employee handbook on my desk computer. "When did you submit your request for your vacation?"

"Back in February," she answered. "The first week of February, I think."

"Okay." I clicked around until I found the vacation policies. They differed according to position, length of employment, and department.

"I don't mean to be a pain in the ass, but this is more than a simple vacation," Beverly pleaded. "I'm going to visit my sick grand-"

"Beverly, you do not have to justify to anyone why you're taking vacation," Lucia bit out. "We all get vacation hours and should be allowed to use them when we want. Especially, if you put the request in over two months ago. Jesus."

"She's right, Beverly," Jeremiah added. "Do not feel bad about feeling like you need to take this next step to take your vacation."

"Okay, I found it," I announced, getting happier the more that I read through the policy that pertained to Beverly. "It reads here that Margo and/or H.R. need to give you a least a month's notice in advance, prior t cancelling your vacation."

Beverly's face lit up. "Really?"

I kept reading, and a part of me was ecstatic at being able to slap Margo in the face with the company policy. "Yes. It states that we can *ask* you t move your vacation, but it is completely up to you if you want to or not. I you do move it due to business needs, the company is also obligated to refun you any monies already paid towards your vacation." I looked up at he "Beverly, your vacation is in two weeks. Margot is past the deadline t cancel." I waited for her to absorb that before asking, "Do you want to canc or not?"

She looked around at all of us as she sadly asked, "Will it make me loo like a big wimp if I say that I'm scared to not cancel and just want my mone back at least?"

Just when I'd thought that I had calmed down, Beverly's words fired m up again. It was completely unacceptable for an employee to be *scared* to tak their earned vacation.

It was utterly ridiculous.

Margot was utterly ridiculous.

"Don't worry about it, Beverly," I answered. "I'll talk to her and tell he that you're taking your vacation per policy. If she wants to fire me, then fuc it, she can fire me. I am so sick of her shit."

Beverly's eyes rounded. "Callie, I don't want you-"

I held my hand up to stop her. "Beverly, this isn't about you. Not reall This is me simply questioning how much longer I can work here," I assure her. "If Margot fires me…well, then she simply saves me from having t decide."

"She's not going to fire you, Callie," Jeremiah insisted. "She's not th; stupid. She knows you have enough stuff to make corporate look in he direction if the H.R. Manager of a division is fired."

I smiled at Jeremiah. "I don't even think I care anymore, Jay," I sai honestly. "Her Godzilla impression this morning really took the cake. Usuall she only goes after a couple of us. Today, she was out of control. It's lik she's fucking mad with power."

Lucia stood up. "Well, I got your back, Callie, if this goes to the point c termination," she offered. "There's no way I'm going to trade you for her."

"Me, too," Brent joined in.

"Same here," Beverly added.

Jeremiah winked at me. "You know I always got your back, babe."

I smiled at them all. "Thanks, guys. I really appreciate that." I really did. "Now why don't we all get back to work before she finds out that we're all i here and decides to just toss in a grenade and be done with us all." They a laughed as I hoped they would.

I walked them all out, and it wasn't until everyone was farther down the hall that Jay turned back towards me and said, "You do know that I got you, right?"

I leaned in, then did something that I'd never done at work before. I brushed my lips across his cheek and fell into the arms already surrounding me. "I know, Jay," I whispered into his chest. "You're a real friend."

"I'm the best kind of friend," he quipped, then kissed me on top of my head. Once he let go of me, I shut the door to my office as he followed the others down the hall and back to his office.

I walked over to my desk, then threw myself down on my chair, wondering how this was going to play out.

Margot was insane.

Pure and simple, she was a fucking lunatic.

So, me going up against her was not going to end amicably. There was going to be guaranteed bloodshed, for sure. Still, I couldn't not help Beverly. It didn't matter if Beverly was my favorite person or not; it was wrong.

Margot was wrong.

Margot was wrong, and I couldn't be scared to do my job anymore.

I spent the next hour gathering up all the vacation policies and proof of Beverly's request and timeline. After that, I called Margot's assistant, Charlotte, and insisted that she pencil me in for a meeting with Margot late this afternoon.

If I was going to have a showdown with her, I'd rather it be at the end of the day, so that I could go home and wash off the blood that I was sure she was going to draw.

Fuck. My. Life.

CHAPTER 12
Happy Wednesday!

Theo ~

My hand automatically reached out for the nightstand in search of my phone
I wasn't sure what time it was, but I knew that it was the middle of th
goddamn night.

Fuck.

However, such was the life of a detective.

I grabbed my phone, saw that it was three in the morning, then put it t
my ear. "Marsden," I answered.

"Get up, kid." I immediately recognized Jason Hansen's voice. He was
veteran beat cop and had no aspirations to move up, but he was damn goo
at his job.

I switched on the nightstand lamp as I sat up. "Whatcha got, Jason?"

"I'm downtown at the Melko building," he informed me. "Caucasian, lat
fifties, female, and dead as a doornail."

"Jesus," I muttered. "Okay. Did you call Franklin yet?"

"He's my next call after I hang up with you," he replied cheerfully.

"Okay. I'm on my way."

"You know the address?"

"Yep," I assured him. "See you soon."

I got out of bed, pissed, washed my face, then brushed my teeth. I thre
on my customary button-up and slacks, holstered my gun, grabbed my key
then made my way towards downtown.

I wasn't all that familiar with the Melko Corporation, but I knew enoug
to know that they dealt in medical technologies or something of that natur
Also, when dealing with medical breakthroughs and millions of dollars i
research and development, it gave anyone a million and one reasons to o
somebody.

I pulled up to the front curb of the building, and just like you'd expect, th
entire street was blocked off within a one block radius. I weaved my wa

through the barricades, then entered the building.

I saw Darren talking to one of the patrolmen, and he cut his conversation short when he spotted me, meeting me in the middle of the lobby. "Happy Wednesday," he chuckled.

"What a coincidence," I remarked drolly, "I was just thinking the same thing." I shot him a look. "Have you been up? What do we have?"

He jerked his head, indicating that I follow him. We made our way to the elevator, then he hit the button for the top floor. "Nah, waiting on you, Stud."

Darren had been calling me Stud since we first partnered up. I wasn't sure why, and I hadn't ever bothered to ask. However, the wait for me was routine. Darren and I thought differently, and that's what made us such a remarkable team. It wasn't anything that we bragged about, but we always closed a majority of our cases.

We had a style and a method that worked for us. We always walked into a crime scene together, then we'd stand and survey the entire area as far as we could see, each of us absorbing different nuances of this or that. We'd compare notes later and fit our observations together like a puzzle of sorts.

When the elevator doors opened, we were immediately greeted by the standard crime scene tape, blocking off all access. We ducked underneath it, then took our time surveying the area. Most of the patrol cops knew this about us, and they always respectfully waited until we were done before they descended upon us with what they had.

A few minutes later, Jason Hansen was walking towards us to give us the scoop. He extended his right hand, and I took it and shook, right after Darren shook it first. "Good to see you boys, but not, ya know what I mean?"

Darren smirked, and I gave him a head nod. "What you got, Jase?"

He sighed. "Just like I told you on the phone, Theo, but with a little more fanfare."

"Fuck," Darren mumbled.

Yeah. Fuck.

"Alright," I sighed. "Lead us to the vic."

Darren and I followed Jason through a maze of walls-not-walls. The entire floor was made up of glass walls instead of traditional drywall. I could make out a conference room, two individual offices, a break room, and one enormous office that took up most of the floor space. Over to the left of the break room was the only private room on the floor. My guess was that it was the restroom.

We came to a halt in front of the main office room, and sure as shit, there was our body. Darren and I took our observations in silence and noted everything that we saw as the M.E. was making her own observations and taking her own notes.

After a few minutes, I asked her, "What do you think?"

Darlene Glines went on the automatic. "Stab wounds running into the tens. I won't know for sure how many until I get her home, but there's at leas twenty so far, in my estimation."

Darren let out a low whistle. "So, a crime of hate or passion," he stated t no one in particular.

Darlene grimaced. "I'm inclined to agree because it gets worse."

My brows rose. "Worse than being stabbed to death over twenty times?"

She glanced up at Darren. "Help me with the body," she instructed, tellin Darren exactly where to touch and how to lift, something that we'd don before when working with her. Even though we had gloves on, we still had t be careful.

When Darlene and Darren angled the body upward a bit, I saw it. "Is tha a-"

"Yep," she said, popping the 'p'. "A rather impressive-sized dildo shove in her rectum."

"Jesus fucking Christ," Darren swore under his breath.

"Okay, so the odds just went up in favor of this being personal, yeah?"

Darlene sent me an incredulous look. "Ya think, Marsden?"

"Fuck," I muttered. "Anything else?"

"Yeah," she answered. "The word 'cunt' is written in black Sharpie marke across her chest."

Darren followed Darlene's lead in positioning the body back to its origin state before standing up. "Okay, so we have hate, for certain. Howeve possibly sexual, indicating a lover or stalker."

I waved Jason over, then asked, "I see her purse marked as evidence, s what do we know about her?"

"Margot Livingston, fifty-eight-years-old, five-ten, 137 pounds, blond hair, blue eyes. Lives over in Palasco." Darren let out another low whistl Palasco was an expensive, uppity, gated residential community. "Of cours that's if her driver's license is current with its information."

"What else?"

"She's the top dog of Melco's Northern California Division. I got th from the cleaning staff who discovered her."

I called over to Darlene, "Time of death?"

"I'd say five to six hours ago," she called back, still engrossed in he examination of the body.

"So, she was killed around ten or eleven, and she was laid up here until th cleaning crew came in at…"

Jason looked at his handheld notebook. "They spotted the body at aroun two. They have strict instructions to clean up here between the hours of tw and six a.m. only."

I looked over to where they had the cleaning crew sequestered. "It's you turn to deal with the tears this time, Dar," I reminded him.

"Goddamn it," he grumbled.

We spent the next two hours interviewing both janitorial ladies, talkin with Darlene and Jason some more, canvassing the entire top floor for cameras or any kind of surveillance set up-to which there was none, much to our surprise-then walking the floor below. We also waited patiently for Darlene and her crew to haul the body out and let the crime scene techs do their thing.

I already knew this case was going to be a bitch. DNA was going to be bullshit because the techs were going to find it *every-fucking-where*. This was a building that employed thousands of people. Anything that the techs found could probably be argued away by any half-ass decent attorney.

I turned to Darren. "I didn't see any kind of key restricted access on these doors or the elevator, did you?"

"Nope," he confirmed. "However, I did see them on the floor below us."

I nodded. I had seen them, too. I called over to Jason. "Hey, Jase?"

"Yeah?"

"Do me a favor and ride the elevator down to each floor and check to see if the other floors have key restricted access."

Jason nodded. "Sure thing."

Darren looked over at me. "Wanna dance down fifteen flights of steps with me?"

Like I had a fucking choice?

"Yeah, yeah…"

We walked down the stairwell and noted anything out of the ordinary. Unfortunately, nothing seemed amiss. Nope. No flashing neon sign telling us who the killer was.

When we reached the lobby floor, I noticed the crowd gathering outside. I was sure that most of it consisted of employees arriving for work, but what I hadn't expected to see was a short, curvy, sexy brunette whose body should still carry the proof of what it felt like to ride my cock.

"God-fucking-damn it." Darren's brows shot up as he looked over at me. I jerked my chin towards the window. "She looked familiar?" Darren's eyes widened when he noticed Callie. "Yeah, talk about fucked."

CHAPTER 13

This was not good.

Theo ~

It still surprised me how pissed off I'd felt when I'd woken up Saturda
morning and had found Callie gone. Intellectually, I'd known that Friday nigh
had all the makings of a one-night stand, but the sex had been so fuckin
phenomenal that I'd been confident that she would want to make an entir
weekend out of it.

Man, talk about your ego getting bruised.

I had woken up, reaching for her, and had been met with nothing but col
sheets.

Christ, I'd been pissed.

That irritation had also grown with each empty room that I ha
encountered. When I had finally been left standing in my living room-*alone*-
had taken everything that I had not to abuse my connections and pull he
name up in the police data base. After all, knowing her full name and the cit
she lived in, it wouldn't have been all that difficult to pull up everything that
wanted to know about her and more.

Specifically, her goddamn address and phone number.

Could be it was because she'd been the first woman that I'd ever cu
inside. Could be because her body had driven me to distraction. Could b
because she had made the sexiest sounds that I'd ever heard when she wa
getting her ass fucked. Whatever it was, one thing was for certain; I wante
more from her.

More time, more sex…just *more.*

However, now she was standing outside a murder scene of a case that ha
landed in my lap.

This was not good.

"I'll interview her when the time comes," Darren offered, pulling me ou
of my thoughts. "But we're still going to have to tell Captain."

"I know," I sighed. There could only be one outcome to all of this; I ha to either stay away from Callie or stay away from this case. I couldn't have the two.

Darren jerked his head sideways. "Let's do this, Stud."

We walked out of the building, and it was just as you would imagine it to be. A crowd had gathered, and the patrol officers were doing their best to hold the barricade. I recognized some of the faces that'd been sitting with Callie at Benji's Friday night, and they all had employee badges on display in one way or another. Some had theirs hanging from lanyards around their necks, some had it clipped to their belts, etc., but it was clear that they all worked here.

Fuck.

This was going to suck, and I knew that Callie was probably going to take exception, but I couldn't approach her. Darren had to be the one to speak to her because neither of us wanted there to be *any* hint of impropriety touching this case.

I ignored the reporters and the rubberneckers as I walked over towards the tall, broad, African American gentlemen that I'd seen sitting next to Callie on Friday night. He eyed me as I approached, and he didn't look too happy to see me. I wasn't sure if it was because of curiosity, jealousy, or the fact that I was ignoring Callie.

Nonetheless, I wasn't going to pretend as if I didn't know the man. "I didn't get your name Friday," I started out. "Can I get it now?" I nodded towards his employee badge. "Along with what you do for Melko?"

"Jeremiah Jackson," he clipped out. Yep. He was pissed at me for some reason. "I'm one of the senior project managers for Melko's Northern California Division."

I jotted down his information, completely ignoring his tone. If he was pissed that I was ignoring Callie…well, I'd give him that. There was a good reason for my behavior, but he couldn't know that. However, if he was pissed because I had spent Friday night between Callie's thighs, well fuck him.

"Can you tell me-"

"I've already told you enough," he cut in. "Now it's time for you to tell me what the fuck is going on."

I raised a brow. "That's not how this works, Mr. Jackson."

"Then I have nothing more to say to you," he retorted, staring me down.

"That's fine," I conceded. "You're not the person that I need to speak with anyway. I'm sure the H.R. Manager can fill me in on everything that I need to know."

Jeremiah crossed his arms over his chest and sent me a victorious look. "Does that mean you'll be letting Ms. Callows know what's going on?"

Ms. Callows?

Callie Callows?

Mother. Fuck. Me.

"Callie's Melko's H.R. Manager?" I asked with dread coating my every nerve.

"Yes, *Ms. Callows* is," he replied, stressing her formal name.

Without another word, I turned my back on him, then went over toward Darren who was talking to one of the patrolmen. He looked up at me when walked up next to him. "What gives?"

"Callie's the H.R. Manager at this site," I told him straight, no fuckin around.

"Goddamn it," he hissed. "Of fucking course, she is." Darren eyed me Having been my partner for over seven years and being the only long-term relationship that I'd ever been in, he knew me better than anyone. H dismissed the patrolman, and in a voice that only I could hear, he asked "What's going on in that mind of yours, Stud?"

I hadn't ever lied to Darren, and I wasn't going to start now. "My firs instinct when I saw her standing outside was *not* to ask her about he connection to Melko," I admitted. "It was to drag her off to the neares unoccupied room and fuck her stupid."

Darren ran his hand over his close-knit fade. "Motherfucker," h muttered. There was no heat behind his utterance, but he couldn't be happ to hear my confession. He peered over at me. "Okay. I'll handle th interview," he said, and then pointed a finger in my face. "But you do *not* sa one goddamn word, Marsden. Do you hear me?"

That stung.

I was not used to taking the backseat to anything. Darren and I had alway worked as a team. However, to move further with the interviews, we neede to speak to Callie and find out who worked with the victim. We weren't abou to waste our time interviewing employees who the victim had never engage with. We'd only go down that avenue if nothing else was panning out.

"Yeah," I mumbled. "I hear you."

We walked over towards Callie, and I fell back, letting Darren make th prominent approach. I stood by silently as he smiled at her. "Hi."

She ignored me and kept her green emeralds focused on Darren. "Hi," sh responded, but didn't smile.

"Uh, it's our understanding that you're the H.R. Manager at this location? he asked.

"Yeah," she confirmed. "I'm part of the senior staff under the location boss, Margot Livingston."

Darren nodded at her confirmation. He pushed one of the road barrie aside. "Do you mind coming and speaking with us…"

"Ms. Callows," she supplied. "It's Callie Callows," she clarified, sti completely ignoring me. "What's this about?"

Darren kept his smile in place. "I'll be happy to tell you once we mov somewhere more private, Ms. Callows." Callie hadn't given him permission t use her first name, so that's why he hadn't.

Callie just nodded, then said, "Okay."

She cut through the barriers silently, but I didn't miss how, not only was she completely-*completely*-ignoring me, but she turned and gave Jeremiah a concerned look. Almost as if she were scared and he should be doing something about it.

I could feel my blood start to simmer at whatever their connection was.

Before we'd left Benji's on Friday, she had clearly stated that she was unattached. So, if that were true, what the fuck was Jeremiah Jackson to her? They weren't related by blood, that much was obvious.

Callie followed Darren into the building, and I followed in behind Callie. How fucking ridiculous was it that I was in the midst of a goddamn murder investigation, but all I could focus on was the way Callie's hips were swaying in front of me with each step?

Christ.

All I needed was to start sporting a goddamn hard-on at a fucking crime scene.

Darren led Callie to a secluded corner of the lobby. When he was certain that we were far enough away from any ear hustlers, he smiled back down at her again. "We haven't been formally introduced, Ms. Callows, but I'm Detective Darren Franklin, and you already know my partner, Detective Theodore Marsden." I had to hand it to the man, he hadn't missed a beat and his face was devoid of any awkwardness.

Callie still refused to look over at me. She simply accepted Darren's introductions and asked, "Well, Detective, can you tell me what's going on? My mind's starting to imagine the worst." Darren shot me a quick look, but Callie didn't follow suit. Her eyes were like green lasers, solely centered on Darren's face.

I knew that I was the one who'd started this, but I had a good fucking reason. I was a cop, and this was a goddamn murder scene. The circumstances demanded the upmost of professionalism, even if I was struggling with it. Besides, she was the one who had bailed on me. If anyone should be pissed, it should be me, goddamn it.

Darren cleared his throat before coming clean. "Ms. Callows, Ms. Livingston's been murdered."

CHAPTER 14
Snitches got stitches.

Callie ~

This was a joke.

It *had* to be a joke.

There was no way that this wasn't a goddamn joke.

My hand automatically shot out to touch Detective Franklin's arm in gesture of…well, I wasn't sure what. However, I'd been quick enough to pu it back before I made contact. "Wh…wh…what?"

"I'm sorry to have to tell you this, but Ms. Livingston was found decease earlier by the janitorial crew," he repeated.

My breath hitched, and it felt like there was a boulder on my ches suffocating me.

From the second that Theo had emerged from the building, making a cle and effective effort to ignore me, I'd been upset because his insultin ignorance had been rude and painful.

I'd known that something terrible had happened because I'd watche enough Law & Order to recognize a crime scene. I'd also known that The and his friend from Friday night weren't your average beat cops because the were dressed like detectives. Well…like television detectives, at least.

However, now, with Detective Franklin telling me that Margot was dea Theo and his cold shoulder was the farthest thing from my mind, even if I *ha been* the one who'd snuck out on him Saturday morning.

Margot had been murdered.

Who gave a crap about a one-night stand, really? Granted, it had been a amazing one-night stand, but it was still meaningless and irrelevant whe faced with the knowledge that someone had been murdered; someone you' known.

"Are you okay?" Detective Franklin asked. "Would you like some water something?"

My eyes were still glued to his brown, sharp, knowing gaz

"N…no…uhm, no," I stuttered. "I'm…I'm fine."

"Are you sure?" he asked, his voice full of concern.

I had no idea if he was genuinely concerned for me or if this was how he dealt with all the people he questioned. I appreciated it, nonetheless. "I'm fine," I said again. "Thank you."

He took a deep breath before nodding, accepting my answer. "Okay. Well, Ms. Callows, as the H.R. Manager, I was hoping you could provide us with a list of names of the employees who worked with Ms. Livingston the closest."

It sounded so cold and tactless coming out of my mouth, but I couldn't stop myself. Ignoring his request, I asked, "Ho…how did she die?"

Detective Franklin cocked his head, but he smiled kindly. "I'm not at liberty to discuss the exact details of-"

I nodded my head, stopping him from finishing what I was sure was their standard cop jargon. "No, that's fine," I interrupted. "I understand." Even though I could feel Theo's gaze on me, he had still yet to address me or even speak. However, that was fine by me. I felt more comfortable speaking with Detective Franklin anyway.

"I'm sorry," he said. "I really am."

I shook my head, trying to clear my thoughts. Someone had killed Margot, so I really shouldn't be concerned with what either detective was thinking or their approach. I ignored Detective Franklin's apology, turning my focus back to the matter at hand.

"Besides Margot's secretary, Maxine Phillips, and her assistant, Charlotte Cornwall, she worked mostly with her senior staff only." I wasn't sure how my next words were going to be perceived, but I wasn't going to lie. "Margot didn't…interact much with any other employees. She was a big fan of company hierarchy and chain of command."

"Are you willing to give us the names of her senior staff?" Detective Franklin asked.

I didn't see any harm in it. It wasn't anything that they couldn't find out on their own anyway. "There…there's me, uhm, Jeremiah Jackson. He's a senior project manager. Lucia Mendez is a senior department manager. Brent Elliot is another senior project manager." I noticed in my peripheral that Theo's pen was whipping across his notebook. Detective Franklin's was as well. "Beverly Sparks is also a senior project manager. Carmen Randall is the senior finance manager. Cody Buckner is another senior department manager. And Ryan Jones is the senior division manager. He worked with Margot the most."

Once Detective Franklin was done with his notes, he eyed me again and asked, "And would you say that you guys all got along fairly well?"

I thought back to Monday's staff meeting, back to when everyone had been in my office venting, and then back to the showdown I'd had with Margot over Beverly's vacation.

No fucking way did we all get along.

Still, snitches got stitches.

I wasn't about to cloud their opinions of the team with *my* opinions of th team. It was unfair, and I was honest enough to know that my views wei biased based on how well I got along with Lucia, Jay, and Brent.

This was *murder* that we were talking about. I was not going to let m opinions help point the finger at anyone. Besides, the whole world hated he Anyone could have killed Margot, from the kid who bagged her groceries t the nuns who practiced at the corner church.

Margot was *evil.*

Who finally did her in was anyone's guess.

I kept my attention focused on Detective Franklin and delivered an answe that he was not going to appreciate. "Sorry, Detective, but this is the pai where I tell you that I'm done with your questioning unless you choose t make this a formal interview. In which case, I'd invoke my right to a attorney." Detective Franklin's face was a perfect picture look of disbelief. H was probably thinking…*and here we'd been, getting along so well.*

After a few seconds of silence, he finally spoke. "Are you serious?"

"Yes, sir," I replied firmly.

That's when Theo finally decided to speak up, and it didn't improve th situation in the slightest. "Callie, this is a goddamn murder investigation," h hissed between clenched teeth. "Do you get that?"

I finally acknowledged him, and I wish that I hadn't. He was just as gooc looking as he'd been on Friday night. He'd been all bad-boy-hot in his jean and Henley shirt at Benji's, but in dress slacks and a button-up, Theo Marsde was simply too fucking stunning for words.

The asshole.

"Make no mistake, Detective Marsden." *I'd be fucked if I was going to call hi Theo.* "I'm very aware of what this is." His jaw clenched. "And because I a very aware of the seriousness of…*this,* I do not feel comfortable influencin your opinion of my co-workers with what I *think* their relationship wit Margot was like."

Theo narrowed his eyes at me. "Callie, your opinion is not importar enough to influence us to see what's not there or ignore what is," he spa "We're professionals, and we've been doing this a long time. Now just answe Darren's question."

This jackass.

"I *did* answer him, Detective," I pointed out.

Theo stepped to me, completely ignoring Detective Franklin's attempt t push him back. "Is this because I didn't go outside and take you in my arms? he growled down at me. "Grow up, Callie. We're talking fucking *murder* here.'

Gone was the Theo that I'd met on Friday night. Standing before me wa Detective Theodore Marsden, and guess what? Detective Theodore Marsde was a fucking asshole.

I straightened my spine, and with thoughts of how serious this situatio was, I leaned into him and said, "Go fuck yourself, Detective."

This sonofabitch stepped further into my space before replying, "I don't have to, *Ms. Callows*. That's what I have *you* for."

Before I could swing on this asshole, Detective Franklin jumped in between us, placed his palms on Theo's chest, then pushed him back. *"Theo,"* he hissed.

Screw this shit.

I might not have liked Margot, but I'd never known anyone who'd been murdered, and even as hot as my temper was, I was still shaken up. I didn't need Theo's bullshit, no matter how great he was in the sack. Theo Marsden didn't have the only nine-inch dick in the world.

I turned from both those fuckheads-*okay, I didn't know if Detective Franklin was a dickhead or not, but he was by association right now*-then stormed out of the lobby doors in search of Jeremiah. As much as I liked Lucia and Brent, Jay was the only person that I trusted completely.

He was still being held back with the throng of other employees, reporters, and all-around nosey people, but because he was so tall, I was able to find him easily. I pushed through the cops and barriers, and not caring how it looked to everyone, I fell into his open arms.

"Are you okay, Cee Cee? What's going on?" he asked, kissing the top of my head.

It wasn't until Jay asked the question that I realized I was shaking. I didn't want to say the words that were going to make this real. I mean, I knew that it was real…but…but sharing it would make it *really* real.

I pulled back, then looked up at him. I couldn't disguise the fear in my voice or the tears brimming in my eyes. "Margot's dead, Jay," I whispered.

His eyes rounded in shock. *"What?"*

"She's gone, Jay," I whispered again. "She's gone. Someone killed her."

CHAPTER 15

Did you fall in love or something?

Theo ~

Darren's body blocking mine was the only thing that kept me from goin
after Callie and dragging her back by her motherfucking hair.

"Theo," Darren snarled. "Get it the fuck together, man."

I stepped back as I ran my hands through my hair. I knew that it was ba
form for me to appear as if I was losing my shit in the middle of a crim
scene, but fuck it, I was.

First, she'd fucking snuck out on me. Second, she ended up being part of
goddamn case. Third, she told me to go fuck myself, then ran off into th
arms of that sonofabitch. It'd been *me* that'd been balls-deep in her ass o
Friday.

Me.

Then she had the nerve to be comforted by another man right in front c
my goddamn face?

"Jesus fucking Christ, Theo. What's your damage, man?" Darren snappec
bringing my attention back to him.

I took in a deep breath, then let it out slowly. "She's making me fuckin
crazy," I confessed.

"I can see that," he retorted, his voice full of sarcasm. "But, fuck, man.
mean, is her pussy that fucking magical that-"

"Do not finish that sentence, Dar. *Do. Not,*" I growled.

His eyes widened, but then he just shook his head. "This is so fucked-up,
he muttered.

My blood was still boiling, but I was finally able to calm my breathing an
get it together. "I know."

Darren let out a deep breath of his own. "Well, we've only interviewed th
janitorial crew and had some preliminaries with Darlene. Let's finish up her
then go talk to Captain," he suggested. "There's no way that he's going t
keep us on this, Stud. You know that, right?"

I dragged my hands down my face. "Yeah, I know," I mumbled.

Jesus Christ.

Callie really was making me fucking crazy. I'd been a cop for over ten years, and I hadn't ever lost my shit like I'd had with her earlier. Even during my rookie years, when I hadn't known shit about shit, I'd still been able to manage some sense of professionalism. However, Callie had me all fucked-up. Maybe Darren was onto something, and her goddamn pussy really was magical. I knew that her sweet ass was.

Still, no matter the cause of my mental meltdown, I owed Darren an apology. We were supposed to be professionals, and I'd let that priority slip through the cracks the second that I'd seen Callie standing outside.

The second that I'd been reminded that she had snuck out on me Saturday morning.

I looked over at Darren. "I'm sorry, Dar. I-"

He was already waving away my apology. "Save it, Stud," he chuckled. "Just know that I expect to be the Best Man at your wedding."

I scoffed as I rolled my eyes. "Seriously?"

Darren smiled. "Theo, I've been your partner for over seven years. We came up the ranks at the same time, and we've been through some shit," he reminded me. "But I have never seen you react to *anyone* this way before. Granted, I'm not around when you're knee-deep in pussy, but I've never known you to lose your shit over a woman." He wasn't lying.

I'd spent all my younger years competing with the best of the best to move up quickly. Women had always been just stress relievers; a small moment of pleasure. Because I'd always been so focused on my career, I also hadn't ever bothered with having a girlfriend. I'd always known that the hours I kept and the commitment to the job would always come first. Hence, why Callie had been the first woman that I had ever ditched a condom for. Hell, I hadn't even ditched it for *her.* I'd done it because she had just felt so goddamn good.

"Be that as it may, Dar, marriage?" I asked. "Did you or did you not just see her tell me to go fuck myself?"

He patted my arm. "She'll calm down," he predicted. "You'll be able to work it out once Holland takes us off this fucked-up case."

I wasn't so sure. However, I knew that I had to table whatever was going on between me and Callie for the moment. Even if the case was going to be yanked from us, we still had to hand over an accurate and detailed pass down report. So, that being said, Darren and I got back to work and gathered as much preliminary information as we could.

Right before we were getting ready to leave, a patrolman called us over to a man who claimed to be Margot Livingston's righthand man, and Ryan Jones had been way more forthcoming that Callie had been. Since his name was on the list of names that Callie had provided, we listened to what the man had to say.

By the time we were ready to leave, Ryan had given us quite a bit and had contacted Melko's corporate offices to inform them of what had happened.

Darren and I had left, but we had some of the patrolmen stay behind fc further observations and questioning.

When we got back to the station, Darren and I didn't waste any tim dicking around. We went straight to the captain's office to report.

His door wasn't closed, so Darren and I walked right in, Darren shuttin the door behind us, and rightfully so. Even though secrets were nonexister in a precinct, I still didn't want my business out there for the world to see.

Or mock.

Captain Everett Holland looked up at us as we sat down in the seats tha were stationed in front of his oak desk. "So, whatcha got, fellas?"

Everett was a big man with a kind smile but a hardened heart. He'd been cop for over twenty years, and it was to be expected that he'd be a littl emotionally malfunctioned by now. Hell, I assumed most cops ended up tha way. He was a petite six-foot-five-inches, still fit, but signs of a little bell pooch were starting to show. His head was covered in a mop of white an silver, but his clean-shaven face showed little signs of his age, which wa surprising, considering he was in his late fifties and the job that he had.

He was also a hell of a boss; fair, direct, and honest as hell.

"A clusterfuck," I answered honestly.

His brows rose as Darren took over. "White female, late fifties, stabbed t death with the word 'cunt' written in permanent marker across her chest and dildo shoved up her ass."

Captain Holland let out a deep breath. "Well, hell," he muttered.

"It gets worse," I warned him.

His keen blue eyes met mine. "It gets worse than having a dildo shoved u your ass?"

"It's worse when the dildo is shoved up *your* ass," I elaborated.

He smirked. "Good point," he chuckled. "So, enlighten me, Marsder How's it worse?"

"The victim was Margot Livingston, and she was the boss of the Melk Northern California Division," I informed him.

"So, the boss," he mulled over. "Depending on the kind of boss she wa the entire building might have wanted her dead, is that it?"

Darren spoke up. "We did manage to speak to the H.R. Manager, and sh gave us a list of the employees that the victim worked with most. We wer also able to speak to one of those people on the list, a Ryan Jones. He sai that the victim was basically a super bitch and was equally hated by ever employee in the building."

Captain Holland let out a low whistle. "No wonder you guys feel lik you're screwed. That *is* a clusterfuck."

I placed my elbows on my knees, clasped my hands together in front c me, then leaned forward. "It *is* a clusterfuck," I agreed. "But that's not th metaphorical dildo that I was referring to, Captain."

"Jesus, there's more?" he asked, his brows reaching for his hairline.

"Yeah," I sighed deeply. "While we were canvassing the lobby, we took notice of a lot of the employees outside reporting for work this morning." He nodded for me to continue. *God, this sucked.* "Well, there was someone…familiar in the crowd, and she happened to be the H.R. Manager for Melko that Darren mentioned earlier."

Captain set his arms on his desk, leaning forward. *"She?"*

Darren sat quietly while I came clean. "I may or may not have met her on Friday night at Benji's, Captain." I leaned back, then shrugged a shoulder. "And I may or may not have invited her back to my place…where she might have spent the night."

Darren busted out laughing when, out of all that, Captain Holland commented, "You actually took this woman back to *your place,* instead of a hotel? What? Did you fall in love or something, Marsden?"

I was not amused. "Can we focus, please," I deadpanned.

He cracked a smile but got serious. "Okay, okay," he said. "Obviously you guys can't take this case on the chance that Marsden's fallen for a potential murderer."

Darren finally got serious. "It's not her, Captain," he voiced with conviction. "Her surprise was genuine when I told her about the victim." Darren shook his head. "You can't fake that kind of shock."

"Yes, you can," he argued. "But I trust your instincts, Franklin." He leaned back in his chair. "Okay, hand the case over to Ridley and Horrace." He waved us away. "Now go do what you guys do." We stood up, then walked out of his office.

Once we got to our desks, I thanked Darren again. "Thanks, man."

He didn't even bother looking up from his notes. "I already told you. As long as I'm the Best Man at your wedding to the firecracker, it's all good."

CHAPTER 16
Seriously, snitches get stitches.

Callie~

The office was officially shut down for the rest of the week. Since we wer
primarily an administrative division, Corporate felt like the reports an
paperwork could hold off for a few days. A handful of vice presidents an
some upper echelons had arrived to deal with the police, the investigatior
and the aftermath of Margot's office being a crime scene.

I still couldn't wrap my mind around the fact that someone had kille
Margot. I mean, I completely understood why somebody would *want* to, bu
to *actually* kill her?

That was completely insane.

Corporate H.R. had stepped in and sent out all the appropriate email
informing all the employees of how the situation was going to be handled, s
I wasn't any more in the know than the rest of the employees.

I was also thankful for it, too.

I wanted *nothing* to do with a murder investigation.

Jesus, when I thought back on how we had just joked about all the way
that we'd like to see her dead, it made my gut tighten. Would we all b
suspects now? I mean, it was bound to get out how that distastefu
conversation had happened. If nothing else, simply because Cody didn't knov
how to keep his mouth shut.

I looked up as Jeremiah set my cup of tea down on the coffee table. "Yo
know, this is my house," I remarked sardonically. "Shouldn't I be the on
getting *you* something to drink and making *you* feel at home?"

Jay chuckled as he sat his fine ass down in one of the mismatche
armchairs that made up the furniture in my condo. "We're too close for tha
kind of hospitality, Cee Cee." He winked at me. "Besides, I'm not the on
who almost got arrested for assault on a police officer," he smirked. "
detective, no less."

I rolled my eyes as I reached for my tea. Returning to my comfortable spc on the couch, I replied, "There's no way he would have pressed charges."

Jay laughed. "Because your bedroom skills are just that bangin'?"

I flipped him off. "No, smartass," I retorted. "He wouldn't have pressed charges because then he'd have to recite in court what he said to deserve the ass whooping."

Jeremiah studied me from over the rim of his coffee cup. I never could understand the public's love for coffee. I preferred water or tea. "You know, Callie-"

"Ugh, what?" I set my tea back down.

The corner of his lip lifted. "I'll admit that I was pissed as all fuck when I saw him ignoring you yesterday." Jay shrugged. "It looked like he had enjoyed himself with you, then decided he no longer had any use for you. Hell, I wanted to punch the motherfucker myself."

"Well, why the hell didn't you?" I complained like a brat.

"Probably because, unlike you, I would have been arrested for assault on a police officer, you twerp." He set his coffee cup next to my teacup on the coffee table. "But after you told me what he said, well…."

I crossed my arms over my chest. "Well, what?"

"Callie," Jay said, stressing my name like I was slow in the head. "He said that was what he had *you* for." He looked at me expectantly. When I didn't comment, he sighed dramatically, again, like I was slow in the head. "That implies that he plans on sleeping with you again, you nutjob."

"How do you figure?" I asked, slightly perturbed.

"Because he said that's what he *has* you for, not that's what he *had* you for," he clarified with that expectant look still plastered on his pretty face. However, I didn't want to talk about Theo because I was still pissed and a little confused. A one-night stand should not have brought forth so much drama. That was the point of one-night stands.

Besides, I didn't want to read too much into what Jay was saying. The truth was simple; no matter the harsh exchange between us earlier, my body hadn't forgotten what it felt like to be taken by Theo Marsden. Hell, the marks on my body were barely starting to fade.

"Who cares about Theo?" I asked flippantly. "We have much bigger issues to discuss, don't you think?"

Jeremiah fell back against the chair. "I still can't believe it."

I grabbed one of the throw pillows off the couch, then hugged it to my chest. "I know it's real, but it still doesn't *feel* real," I tried to explain. "You know what I mean?"

He nodded. "Nonetheless, I tell you what," he said, shuttering. "I'm happy as fuck that my Margot death wish was an evil wraith extracting her spine from her body and nothing plausible."

"Thankfully, all the stories were pretty farfetched," I agreed. We still didn't know the details about her death. So far, all we'd gotten was a confirmation of a stabbing by the local news anchor's secret source. Other than that, we knew nothing.

"I just don't know how to feel about it all, Jay," I admitted.

Jeremiah shot me a look. "Oh, puhlease, Callie," he scoffed disdainfully. "Margot Livingston was a vile, world-class, cow-cunted bitch. No one is sorry that she's gone."

"Jay," I admonished.

"It's the truth," he insisted. "It's only talking ill about the dead if you're lying or talking shit. I'm doing neither. I'm speaking facts. And the fact is that she was a horrible human being, and everyone's only concern is *who* did it, not *why*."

He was right.

I knew he was right, but it still seemed like poor form. "Granted, I agree that no one will probably miss her, but she still didn't deserve to be murdered, Jay," I said wryly.

Jay let out a sigh. "I'm not saying that she did," he clarified. "I'm just saying that the odds are that no one is sad to see her go, is all." Then he went on to shock the shit out of me. "I think Ryan did her in."

My back straightened as I gaped at him. *"What?"*

He shrugged a shoulder carelessly, then explained, "Think about it. He's been missing for the past three weeks or so. He's been spending most of his time behind closed doors with Margot, missing staff meetings and team communication meetings."

"So?" Yeah, Ryan sightings have been scarce lately, but it was a far leap from him just being busy to outright murdering Margot.

"Maybe they were working on a secret project, and she double-crossed him," Jeremiah suggested. "Or maybe they were secret lovers, and they had a falling out, and so he killed her in a jealous lover's rage."

I could feel my eyes bugging out of my head. "Dude, you watch way too much Investigation Discovery," I said, throwing a pillow at him.

He caught it expertly as he retorted, "It's possible, Cee Cee." I wanted to tell him that he was crazy, but I couldn't. Last week, if anyone had told me that Margot was going to be murdered, I would have told that person they were crazy, too, and look where we're at now.

However, I was favoring Jay's theory that they were working on a secret project, and she double-crossed Ryan over the secret lovers thing. Ryan Jones was a good-looking sonofabitch. He could do way better than Margot Livingston. Unless, of course, he'd been sleeping with her for an ulterior purpose.

Then Jay got seriously serious. "What are you going to say when they question you about Friday night?"

I'd thought about that a lot since yesterday, and my stance still hadn't changed on that particular subject. We were all guilty of participating in that conversation, and no matter how I felt about any of the people in attendance Friday night, I wasn't saying shit.

Seriously, snitches got stitches.

"I don't know what you mean, Jay," I sing-songed. "I was drinking and taking tequila shots. I couldn't tell you who said what. As a matter of fact," I stressed, my face overtaken by my smile, "I was so drunk that I actually went home with a stranger that night and did the most unspeakable of things."

Jeremiah stared at me for a second before he finally threw his head back and laughed. I just continued to grin at him as he got himself under control. "Jesus Christ, woman," he said through his chuckles. "You are something else, Callie Callows."

When we were done laughing at my absurdness, I said, "Seriously, Jay. I'm not a snitch. We *all* hated Margot, and we *all* spoke of her wishful demise freely. I'm not going to steer the police in anyone's direction. We're either all guilty or innocent in our equal hate for that woman."

He nodded his head in agreement. "You're right. Besides, it's not our job to do the cops' jobs for them. They can figure it out on their own." With that, he stood up, then walked over to me, placing a kiss on the top of my head. "I gotta go, but I'll call you later."

I looked up at him. "Okay," I said, smiling. I didn't walk him to the door because what he'd said earlier was true; we were too close for guest hospitality. So, I kept my lazy ass on the couch.

Jeremiah had his hand on the doorknob, ready to shut the door behind him, when he turned back at me and said, "You know I love you, right?"

"Yep," I teased, popping the 'p'.

"So, don't get all violent on me when I tell you that I think you should give your detective a second chance," he said, surprising the hell out of me. "No man gets that possessive over a one-night stand, crazy girl." Then the bastard shut the door before I could call him ten different kinds of a traitor.

I laid back on the couch, then studied the ceiling like it had the answers to all my problems. However, just in case you were wondering, it didn't.

CHAPTER 17
What are you doing here?

Callie ~

A knock at the door had me pausing Takers. I'd seen the movie a millio
times, but with a cast as hot as this, I never got tired of this movie. My ovarie
had this movie on repeat.

So, I'd like to think that, had I not been distracted by a cast that include
Matt Dillion, Hayden Christensen, and Michael Ealy, I would have paid bett
attention to the time. I would have wondered at someone knocking at m
door so late in the evening.

I would have looked out the goddamn peephole.

Nevertheless, I hadn't.

I swung open the front door to my condo and stared up into the face c
Theodore Marsden, Asshole Detective.

It took me only half a second to snap out of my shock, and when I did,
went to slam the door shut, but Theo had been ready for it. He slapped h
hand against the wood, then pushed it open, forcing me to back up or b
smacked by my own front door.

What a jackass.

I stared in disbelief as he walked straight into my living room as if he'
been invited, and when I finally found my voice, I shrieked, "Get the hell ou
of my house."

Theo looked imposing as he stood in the middle of my living room, an
for a split second, I wondered about my home through his eyes.

I'd grown up with parents who had shunned material possessions and sti
did. Now, they weren't fanatics or anything like that, they'd just been olde
and had a different view on life.

I'd been an 'oops baby', but my parents had never made me feel that wa
They loved me and had provided for me the best way they'd known how
They were just very unconventional.

We had lived in a small trailer in your average trailer park, and while I' had all the necessities, my parents had spent their extra money on trips and adventures for me versus the latest gaming system or fancy jeans. When I had graduated high school, college had been an option that they'd had no opinion on. They had just wanted me to be happy, they'd said.

Still, I had chosen to go to college, and the day that they had safely tucked me away in my dorm at Stanford, my parents had moved out of our trailer, bought a brand spanking new RV, and they haven't stopped traveling since.

My father had been an executive engineer, and my mother had been a corporate accountant. They'd made a very good living, but they'd said working within the 'corporate rat race'-as they had called it-had taught them the value of family over money and quality time over material possessions.

I'd always been grateful for the family values that they had instilled in me, but my upbringing had made me seem a bit quirky to others. Jay was the only one that didn't judge the fact that my furniture didn't match or that I had an aversion to shopping.

It had taken me years to buy my condo, even though I'd had the credit score and income to purchase a home early on. Making a commitment to an inanimate object had been a big move for me. I'd been terrified of making a financial mistake.

So, with Theo standing in my home, I briefly wondered if he was judging it, but then I snapped out of it when I remembered that he was an asshole and that I was mad at him.

He put his hands on his hips and glared at me. "I'm not going anywhere," he growled.

My idiotic, backstabbing, traitorous eyes couldn't help themselves. They took him in and really took notice of how hot the jerkface looked. He was in jeans and a Quicksilver t-shirt with Timberlands, and he looked delicious.

"What are you doing here?" I spewed like a fishwife. "And how the hell do you even know where I live?"

"How the hell do you think?" he replied, his voice still low and gravely. "I did a background check on you, and it told me everything that I needed to know about you."

Shock had me momentarily stunned into silence. This asshole did a *background check* on *me*? After a few seconds, I shouted, *"What?!"*

Theo sighed. "Callie, we run background checks on everyone we question during a murder case. It's standard."

Oh.

Still…

"So, where is Detective Franklin since you're here in an official capacity?" I still had the door swung wide open, and I cringed internally when I realized that my neighbors could probably hear all the drama. Still, I wasn't going to shut the door until Detective Marsden was on the other side of it.

"Who says I'm here in an official capacity?" he retorted.

Okay, *now* that was my cue to be offended. "You…you can't do…do that," I sputtered, my voice back to shrieking status. "You can't use offici[a] police procedure for personal use." I mean, I wasn't a cop or lawyer, but [I] was pretty sure that Theo using his connections for personal benefit wa[s] illegal. At the very least, it was unethical.

He stormed over towards me, grabbed the door right out of my hand[,] then slammed it shut before saying, "Then call the fucking police."

This man was really going to make me catch a court case. I was going t[o] be arrested and have to recount the events leading up to Theo's ass beatin[g] for a courtroom full of people.

"Get out of my house, Detective Marsden," I gritted through clenche[d] teeth.

"Not before you answer a few questions for me, Ms. Callows," he sho[t] back.

Was he deaf? I'd already told him that I wasn't talking. "I'm not a sissy-l[a] la, *Detective*. I will not be persuaded or bullied into doing something I feel isn[']t right."

Theo towered over me with a significant height difference, but I wasn[']t going to cower. "Well, I'm not leaving here until you tell me why the fuck yo[u] snuck out of my bed Saturday morning," he snarled.

Whoa.

Wait.

What?

I blinked up at him.

Then blinked again.

He was here to talk about...*that?*

I placed my hands on my hips. "What the hell are you talking about?"

He narrowed his beautiful, deep, bedroom brown eyes. "Why did yo[u] sneak out of my bed Saturday morning, Callie?" he asked again.

I took exception to his use of the word 'sneak', even though that's exact[ly] what I'd done. "You were sleeping," I answered as casually as I could. "[I] didn't see the point in waking you up."

Theo's jaw ticked, and damn my soul to hell, it was sexy as all get ou[t]. "Why did you leave *period*, Callie?"

Uh, okay...now I was getting confused.

My brows furrowed, and my hands dropped from my hips. "Isn't th[e] one-night stand etiquette 101? The guest leaves the following morning, a[ll] stealthy like, as to not have to endure the morning-after awkwardness?"

He stepped forward until I was forced to step back or be run over. M[y] back hit the wall, but I didn't avert my eyes. I wasn't going to let this jacka[ss] intimidate me. Little did he know, Margot's vicious bullying had prepared m[e] well for the assholes of the world.

"I'm curious, Callie," he said, his voice smooth but full of irritation. "Wh[at] exactly did I say or do on Friday night to give you the impression that w[e] were a one-night stand?"

That whole blinking shock thing? Yeah, I was at it again. "Wh…what?"

"You heard me," he mercilessly snarled at me. "What made you think that we were a onetime thing?"

I snapped out of my minor shock at his tone. He was talking to me like I was stupid, and I didn't appreciate it one bit. "Because you picked me up from a goddamn bar after I'd been drinking and taking tequila shots," I said, stating the obvious. "Because I let you stick your fingers inside me at that same goddamn bar. What other impression of me could you have gotten other than I was the kind of woman who was only good for a one-night stand?" I did avert my eyes then. I hadn't realized how much I revealed until the words had all tumbled out.

"Look at me," Theo growled. When I shot my eyes back to his, he asked, "So, are you telling me that you missed the part when it went from two strangers fucking to something more?"

With my hands back on my hips, I answered, "Are you talking about Monday morning when you completely ignored me when you went outside and only spoke with Jeremiah?"

The tick in his jaw was back, and I could feel my knees weaken a bit. "No," he gritted out. "I'm talking about when my dick was balls-deep inside that tight ass of yours." I gasped. I hadn't expected him to voice that particular act aloud. A gentleman would pretend like that had never occurred. "Because no woman lets a man fuck her up the ass on the first night unless she's a complete whore or the chemistry is so off the charts that it can't be ignored." He leaned down into my face. "And I know for a fact that you're not a whore, Callie."

I had no idea why I did it. When you paid attention to his *actual* words, Theo had actually been hinting to something important and meaningful. He'd been implying that I was the complete *opposite* of a whore. However, his blatant reference to something so…slutty, then paired with an emotionally fucked-up week, I couldn't stop myself.

His head snapped sideways as the slap echoed throughout the condo.

CHAPTER 18

I've never been slapped before.

Theo ~

I'd never been slapped before.

I gotta say…it was an odd sort of feeling.

I mean, yeah, my face stung like a bitch. Plus, with Callie being so short, I hadn't ever expected her to pack such a powerful punch. Of course, I hadn't ever expected her to slap the shit out of me, either. The problem was that I wasn't sure if I deserved it or not.

When she'd given such a crude and lewd account of what had happened between us at the bar, my chest had been hit with a little pang of regret. I hadn't realized that she viewed our encounter under that light, and as the night had worn on, the dirtier the sex had gotten. It wasn't too farfetched for a woman to think that a man might think the worst of her after all the things that Callie had let me do to her body.

Still, I thought that I'd made it clear that I hadn't viewed her or anything that we'd done in that light. I was pretty sure that I'd stressed to her that she *wasn't* a whore.

See, I didn't come from a family of cops or anything like that, a family where we'd all been upstanding, respectable people. My dad had worked at a meat packing plant, and my mom had worked part-time as a librarian for the local elementary school. We'd been a typical middle-class family, a little more near the bottom of that range than the top, and the neighborhood that we'd lived in had been much of the same.

The only difference between my house and the neighbors was that mine had housed a man who'd been a miserable sonofabitch and couldn't find joy in anything he did or experienced.

It'd been the classic sob story of a kid who had excelled in sports but had torn his knee up during his senior year of high school fucking around. He'd been forced to give up all his big aspirations for his future after that.

By then, he'd been already committed to my mother, and she had stood by him during those depressing times. Eventually, he'd started working at the local meat packing plant, and my mother had actually been going to community college until she'd gotten pregnant with me.

To prove that he'd still been the man that he really hadn't been, when my mom had gotten pregnant, he had bullied her into quitting school and becoming a homemaker. Now, there was nothing wrong with being a homemaker if that's what you *chose*. However, my mother hadn't chosen that. Not completely. Still, Craig Marsden's wife was not going to work; she was going to stay home, raise their children, and be a good wife.

So, as the classic story always went, the more miserable that my father had felt, the more abusive he had become. He would beat on my mom whenever he'd felt that the occasion called for it, which admittedly, wasn't all the time. His preferred choice of abuse had been verbal.

This had gone on for years until I'd been old enough, big enough, and strong enough to kick his ass. Though he'd kept on with the verbal insults, he had backed off the physical. Well, that I knew of. Once I'd moved out, I couldn't say what went on between him and my mother. I had no contact with him at all, and I only spoke to my mom randomly, just to check in.

I had ended up becoming a cop because the need to protect people had settled in my soul the first time that I'd ever seen my dad hit my mom. I'd been seven-years-old and the helplessness had been real, and it had cut deep. It's what made me treat all women with respect, whether they deserved it or not. Just like my mom did, I was always mindful that everyone had a story, so I did my best to never mistreat a woman. I was always honest with my intentions, and I never let a woman pull me into her drama.

Until now.

Until Callie.

Now she'd gone and slapped me, and my immediate sense of reaction was to throw her down and fuck her until she saw things my way. However, out of fear for my balls, I decided to nix that course of action.

At least, for right now.

It helped that her precious green orbs were the size of saucers. It was like she couldn't believe that she'd done it.

"Are you done?" I asked, surprised at how calm I sounded when my heart was racing.

"Theo…" she whispered horrified.

Then her words resonated in my head. "What part scares you the most, Callie?" I asked. "That I might think you're easy or that, to me, it wasn't just a one-night stand?"

Callie started wringing her hands together, and her eyes were like ping pong balls, darting around all over the place. I reached up, then took her chin in my hand, forcing her to look at me. She didn't answer me, instead came back with a question of her own. "Why did you ignore me on Monday?"

"Because you might have murdered your boss, Callie," I answered frankly.

"It had to be reported that there was no communication between us. Some people could have deemed it unprofessional or biased."

"What changed?" she asked. "Once we were inside, you didn't have any problem speaking to me. As a matter of fact, some could even say that you caused a bit of a scene."

I ran my hand from her chin, down her slender neck, across her collarbone, then down over her heavy roundness. Her breath hitched, and when I squeezed on her tit gently, Callie let out a low moan. It felt good to know that her body still remembered everything that I'd done to it, no matter how pissed off she was at me.

"Because, by then, I knew that I had to hand over the case to someone else. There's no way Darren and I were going to be able to keep it when I already knew I wasn't going to stay away from you." Her eyelids fluttered, and her lips parted. She might be pissed off at me, and she might have thought of me as a one-night stand only, but there was no denying that Callie still wanted me.

"So, you're not investigating Margot's case anymore?" she asked, her voice low and husky.

Callie was wearing a light blue t-shirt and a pair of green pajama pants with lollipops all over them, perfectly her. Still, all I could think about was how easy it was going to be to rid her of her clothes as I snaked my hand up underneath her shirt, then slid it across her soft skin until I was cupping her bare tit.

God, I fucking loved her big, heavy, teardrop breasts.

I was never going to forget the vision of my cock sliding in between them and watching my dick erupt all over her neck, chest, and tits.

Ever.

I forced my brain to return to the topic at hand. "No," I said, finally answering her. "I told my captain about you, so he reassigned the case to another team of detectives." Her body melted, and her eyes darkened. It was like she'd been given a reprieve from the world's problems.

Her hands reached out until they rested on my hips. Callie closed her eyes and moaned, finally giving in to the sensation of her tit in my hand. When she opened her eyes again, she asked, "So, what does that mean?"

I wrapped my free hand around the back of her neck, then I crushed her to my chest. "It means that you're mine." Her eyes widened, but she didn't argue. "It means that you're mine to do whatever the fuck I want with."

A lot of women might take that as a threat, but Callie took it like I knew she would. She started to pant softly, and I could feel her skin warming in my palm. "And what is it you want to do to me?"

My dick shot to rock hard status the second that I palmed her tit, but her question turned my dick from just hard to painfully desperate. I thought about all the things that I'd done to her on Friday night, and the truth was that there wasn't much else left for us to explore.

I hadn't been exaggerating when I had referred to our chemistry as being off the charts. Sure, there'd been alcohol involved and that had lowered our inhibitions, but the fire that had fueled the cravings, the desires, the unapologetic need…that had all been real.

I ran my hand down from the hold that it'd had on her tit and slid it underneath the waistband of her pajama pants. My hand kept going until I bypassed her panties and my fingers found her soaking warmth. Callie was wet and ready to get fucked.

So, what did I want to do to her? The list of things that I didn't want to do to her was shorter. Still, she was already feeling…weird or regretful about some of her behavior Friday night, so I didn't want to say the wrong thing. Because of that, instead of telling her that I wanted to fuck her like her only purpose in life was to serve the needs of my hands, tongue, and dick, I said, "Whatever you'll let me, Callie."

Her face went from lustful to anxious and her eyes started to swim with confusion. I couldn't lose her now, not to unfounded doubt. I bent my fingers, rubbing on her sensitive g-spot, trying to get her out of her head.

"Oh, God…" Callie moaned.

"Just so you know, baby," I whispered near her ear. "There's nothing I don't want to do to you."

"Theo…"

I upped the tempo of my fingers, drawing out her pleasure. "I want a repeat of everything we did Friday night, Callie," I told her honestly. "All of it. Every pleasure, each sensation, and all the filth…I want it all again." Her hands latched onto my forearm, and she held on as she rode my fingers to orgasm. "I'm not going to lie, Callie. I want to fuck you like you don't have a choice, but I don't want to do anything that's going to make you uncomfortable."

She didn't respond to my comment. Instead, Callie just closed her eyes and let her body spasm all around my fingers. I dropped my head on the wall behind her, then closed my eyes, remembering what it felt like to have her pussy pulsating around my cock.

All women felt different. They smelled different. They responded differently. They were uniquely their own version of the species.

However, Callie? Callie not only felt different, smelled different, and responded differently…she drew me to her in a way no other woman ever had.

I gave up a motherfucking case to be with her.

She was the first and *only* person who I had ever put before my career. If she knew the truth about my obsession with her, she'd get a fucking restraining order against me, and I wouldn't blame her.

After her tremors subsided, she said the one thing that fueled my obsession to depths that gave me chills. "Just ignore me when I say no, then," she whispered. "I won't ever mean it when I'm with you anyway."

I guess Darren was going to be my Best Man after all.

CHAPTER 19

I'd never been kissed like this before.

Callie ~

I meant what I'd said, and I could only hope that my trust in Theo wouldn't be misplaced.

From the second that I'd run into him by the restrooms at Benji's, my body had developed a mind of its own. All sense of rationale and responsibility was foreign or nonexistent. For Christ's sakes, I let the man screw me without any thought to protection. I let him cover me in his seed like a paid whore. I also let him mark me like he owned me.

All on the first friggin' night.

Plus, I wasn't so much in denial not to admit that I wanted what most women wanted. I wanted Theo to fuck me like I was his whore to use any way that he saw fit, but I also didn't want him to think less of me because of it. I didn't want him thinking that I behaved like this with all men. I didn't want him thinking that I didn't deserve to be respected *outside* the bedroom just because I liked my sex dirty.

Still, I didn't want to utter those cringe-worthy words…*'I've never done this before'* or *'you're the only guy I've ever done this with'*. I doubted that he'd believe me anyway. Even if he did, it still sounded a little bit like the lady doth protest too much.

Just when I was letting my insecurities and self-image issues drown me, Theo removed his fingers, sucked them clean, then went and said the one thing that erased all my doubts. "As much as it makes me lose my mind hearing you say those words, you didn't have to tack on the 'with you' part, baby." He smirked down at me. "I know you've never done…been with someone like that before, Callie."

I had to ask how he could know such a thing. "How do you know?"

Theo grabbed my face, then slammed his lips on mine. I opened up for him, then moaned when his tongue swept inside to dance with mine. I reached up, wrapping my arms around his neck at the same time that he released my face to circle his arms around my body, crushing me in his embrace. Theo had my body flushed against his with no breathing room in between.

His mouth slanted over mine, and it was a kiss filled with passion and wicked promises. It was a kiss with the implications of so much more to come.

I'd never been kissed like this before.

When Theo finally broke the connection, he looked down at me and said, "Because that right there, this feeling, this *need*…I refuse to believe that you've felt it before with someone else, Callie." I could feel myself ready to swoon. "Because *I* sure the fuck have *never* felt this way towards another human being in all my life." His words weakened my knees and made me feel special. "There's no way that you've ever let another man touch you the way that you let me on Friday night. No. Fucking. Way."

I ended up saying those cringe-worthy words. Or, at least, I tried to say them. "I've never-"

"I know, baby." Theo kept one hand on my waist as he brought the other one to my face. He ran his thumb back and forth over my bottom lip, and the slutty part of me wished it were his cock. "You think I don't know that your sweet ass was virgin that night?" I blushed, but I didn't stop his dirty dialogue. "You think I don't know that I'm the only man you've ever let paint your face? Leave my fucking teeth marks in your flesh?"

I could feel my body coming alive with each word. "Theo…"

He leaned down and softly kissed my lips. It was a quick, sweet, tender kiss. When his eyes returned to mine, he continued trying to convince me that this was real. "I studied every sound you made, every way your body moved, every expression that danced in your eyes that night. I knew the exact moment you were experiencing something new, Callie. There was no fucking way I was going to let us be a one-night stand."

"So, what are we now?" I didn't want to sound clingy, but everything he was saying screamed out commitment.

The corner of his lips lifted. "I already told you," he answered. "You're mine and that makes me yours, Callie." His words were spiraling me down a rabbit hole that I was pretty certain was going to fuck me over later. "And because you're mine, I'm going to do exactly what you said."

"What's that?"

"I'm going to ignore you every time you play hard to get, and I'm going to fuck you like you were created to be my own personal slut, baby."

My body broke out in shivers, and my core clenched with his dirty predictions. A part of me wondered if there was something wrong with me to like the things he was saying. However, another part of me-the part that knew what he was capable of in bed-didn't care overly much. I also couldn't imagine a scenario where I'd ever say no to him, so I asked, "Promise?"

Theo didn't answer. Instead, he growled, picked me up bride style, then walked me back towards the bedrooms. "Which one is your bedroom, Callie?"

"Down the hall, the last door on your left," I told him breathlessly. Even though he'd already done the most remarkable things to me on Friday night, right now I was sober as a judge, and the anticipation of what was to come, knowing that none of my senses would be dulled by alcohol, had me ready to burst.

Theo sat me down on my bed, then stood before me, aligning his cock right in front of my face. My first instinct was to let him lead, but his earlier words of assurance had me reaching for the button and zipper of his jeans.

His hand sank in between my scalp and the knot of hair thrown on top of my head. He cradled my head as I pushed his jeans and underwear down to his thighs, freeing his deliciously hard cock. Those nine inches of steel looked tight and angry, and damn, did Theo have an enticing dick.

I didn't waste any time with teasing or toying. I leaned forward, then wrapped my lips around the head of his cock, and he tasted just as good as I remembered, all soap, musk, and man.

"Fuck, baby," he groaned as his hand tightened on my scalp. "Your mouth is just as lovely as I remember, Callie." His words were meant to encourage, and they did.

I grabbed the base of his cock and swallowed as much dick as I could. I didn't have the haze of alcohol to loosen me up, so I gagged on his nine inches, but I didn't stop trying to swallow him whole.

Tears were streaming down my face, and I was struggling to breathe, but I was going to blow Theo for all I was worth. "Fucking Christ, Callie," he hissed out. "Suck that cock, baby. Swallow every inch." I couldn't, and he probably knew that I couldn't, but neither of us cared. There'd be plenty of times for me to keep practicing later on.

After a few more minutes of me sucking Theo off, he finally pulled my mouth off his dick. "That's enough," he growled. "The first time is not going to be down your throat. I need inside your pussy, baby."

Theo pulled off his shirt, then removed his shoes and socks, pushing his jeans and underwear the rest of the way down until he was completely naked.

Holy Moly…I didn't think I'd ever get tired of this sight.

He pulled me up, then made quick work of my clothes, and the next thing I knew, we were laying across my bed, Theo's hot, hard, masculine body covering mine, my legs spread open to cradle him. I supposed that he was feeling the same desperation that I was because he skipped all foreplay and entered me in one hard, deep, powerful thrust.

My back arched, my fingers dug into his shoulders, and I moaned out his name. "Theo…"

Theo braced himself on one elbow while he reached back with his other arm, then hooked my knee over his elbow. He opened my body wider and started pounding into me with enough force to make the headboard slam into the wall. "Jesus, fuck, Callie," he grunted. "Your pussy's still as tight as ever." I moaned and let his dirty words play like music to my ears. "And when this tight pussy can't take my cock anymore, I'm going to turn you over on all fours and fucked that ass again, baby."

My body tightened around him, and I wasn't above admitting that I wanted that, too. "Yes," I pleaded. "Please, Theo…"

His thrusts became harder and deeper. "God, you're killing me, Callie," he groaned. "Knowing you like my cock up your ass just as much as I want to give it to you is. Fucking. Killing. Me."

I started lifting my hips, meeting him thrust for thrust, and I just knew that I was going to have bruises again. Still, I didn't care. I didn't care about whatever Theo wanted to do to me because I knew that it was going to feel extraordinary, no matter what it was.

"Theo, make me cum," I begged.

He let out a low growl and started driving into me harder and harder, and it felt like that nine-inch steel pipe was reaching inside me everywhere. "My pleasure," he snarled, then proceeded to do just that.

It wasn't a few thrusts and filthy words later that my body was tightening all around him. *"Theo…"* I screamed out as I shattered around him, pulsing and thrashing about with the intensity of my explosion.

"Oh, God, baby," he hissed right before he slammed into me one more time, twitching and growling, emptying himself inside me.

I couldn't do anything but lay there as Theo dropped his weight on me, then rolled us over, curling me into his side. Our labored breathing was all that could be heard, and my body still trembled with the aftershocks of my orgasm.

Theo Marsden was a goddamn sex god.

I could feel Theo's chest vibrate beneath my cheek. "Thanks, I think."

I cringed. "Sorry, I didn't realize I'd been thinking out loud."

I could feel his body strain as he leaned up to kiss the top of my head. "Don't apologize on my account," he quipped. "I rather like your opinion of me."

The words were out of my mouth before I could stop them. "I rather like you."

Theo rolled over on top of me again, braced his weight on his elbows as he pushed my hair out of my face, then kissed my nose. "And I rather like you, too," he whispered across my lips. "As a matter of fact, I rather like you a lot."

CHAPTER 20
You're leaving me?

Theo ~
My eyes popped open to a sound that I knew as well as my own heartbeat.

There were only four ring tones set on my phone: one for my mother, one for Darren, one for work, and one for regular calls. Though, soon, there'd be five…one for Callie's calls.

Darren's ringtone was chiming from my phone, and this was the first time that I'd ever resented the sound. Normally, I'd be all about work.

I reached over, silencing the ring, not wanting it to wake Callie up. I turned my head, and she was still cradled in my arms, half of her naked body clinging to my side.

I never would have thought it possible, but last night had been unexpectedly ten times better than Friday night. I didn't know if it was because it was understood that we were dating now, or the simple fact that one day away from Callie was one day too damn long, and my body had been just so thrilled to be near her again.

Whatever it was, I hadn't done anything new to her last night, but what we'd done had been filthy, emotional, and powerful. Regardless, whether I was moving too fast for her or not, Callie was mine, end of story.

I meant everything that I'd said to her last night. However, the only thing that I hadn't mention was that, even though the Livingston case had been handed off to another team of detectives, it was still messy for me to be involved with a woman who had direct ties to a murder victim. I tried to ease my conscience by arguing that I wasn't lying to her, so much as just not sharing everything.

Making sure not to wake her, I eased my arms out from under her gloriously naked form, and when she whimpered, I kissed her forehead, lulling her back to sleep.

I climbed out of her bed as quietly as I could, grabbed my phone, then walked naked into her living room. I dialed Darren back, and he answered immediately. "Hey, Stud."

"What's up?" I whispered.

"Why you whis-*ohhhhhh,*" he drawled out, the smile evident in his voice.

"Oh, nothing," I retorted. "What's up?"

He let it go, but I knew that he'd be asking questions later. "I got a call from Chaz Earlmyer. He's ready to talk."

Chaz Earlmyer was a snitch who thought that no one knew he was a snitch. He was always trying to excuse his lack of loyalty, but I didn't care what he told himself to ease his conscience. As long as he gave up the goods, I cared about nothing else. One of our cases was the murder of a nineteen-year-old girl that'd been rumored to be involved with gang drug trafficking, and Chaz's name had come up during some of our interviews.

"Where's he at?" I asked.

Darren chuckled. "The bastard's actually over by MacArthur at a Starbuck's," he answered. Well, props to Chaz. No one would recognize him on the rich side of town. "I…ah, I can go alone if you're busy, Stud."

"Fuck you, Dar," I grumbled. "I can meet you there in twenty." Darren let out a low laugh but didn't comment as he hung up the phone.

Fuck.

The last thing that I wanted to do was leave Callie. I wanted her to wake up in my arms, but in my line of work, it was going to be seldom that she did.

I headed towards the bathroom, shut the door, took a piss, then started opening the drawers, looking for an extra toothbrush. When I found a value pack in the bottom drawer, I picked a toothbrush and claimed it as my own.

After brushing my teeth and placing the toothbrush in the cup holder next to hers, I washed my face and looked for some baby powder or anything that I could use as makeshift deodorant. I found some, and after doing the best I could, I walked back into the bedroom to get dressed.

I wasn't sure how Callie was going to feel about it, but it was obvious that I was going to have to bring some personal toiletries over here since we were going to do this.

After I got dressed, I walked over to the bed, then took in the sight of Callie asleep on her side, her hands curled underneath the pillows. She looked serene, perfect, and too tempting for my sanity.

I leaned over, then nuzzled her neck. "Callie, baby?"

"Mmmmm…" was her only reply as her body adjusted to a more comfortable position.

"Callie, baby?" I repeated. "I have to go."

Her eyelids fluttered open, and it took a second for her green beauties to focus. "Theo?"

I smoothed her tangled, wild, dark brown silk from her face. "Yeah," I said, smiling as I leaned down to kiss her cheek. "I gotta go, baby."

She blinked a few times, trying to wake up and comprehend what I was telling her. Her brows furrowed. "You're leaving me?"

Her words stabbed at my chest. "No," I assured her. "I'm never going to leave you." I ran my thumb across her lower lip. "But I just got a call from Darren," I explained. "Work calls, babe."

Callie closed her eyes as she nodded. She hugged her pillow closer and got comfortable again. "Mkay…" she muttered.

I really, really, really loathed leaving her. "I'll be back later, okay?"

She nodded again, then turned back into her pillow, effectively shutting me out and going back to sleep. I chuckled, kissed her on the cheek again, then made my way out of her condo.

As I walked out of the condominium complex and towards my car, my mind wasn't on my job. It was full of thoughts of exchanging house keys, cleaning out drawers, and making room in each other's closets.

Fuck, I was so goddamn whipped.

I mean, who in their right mind fell to these depths after only a week?

Darren had sent me a text, letting me know where he was parked, so when I pulled up next to his car twenty minutes later, as soon as I shut the door to my car, he wasted no time. "Cleared things up, did you?"

I grunted. "Where's Chaz?"

Darren nodded towards the happily lit Starbucks. Most Starbucks weren't open this late-or early-but when the wealthy needed you open to cater to their caffeinated needs, you opened. "So?"

I knew that he wasn't going to let it go until I gave him something. "We…came to an understanding," I finally answered.

"An understanding, huh?" he smirked.

I let out a sigh. "We're dating," I clarified.

"And if it turns out that she's the one who killed the Livingston woman?"

I cocked my head as I eyed him. "Aren't you the same person that told Captain that your gut says it wasn't her?"

Darren full-on smiled. "Yep, that was me," he answered. "*Buuuuuuut*…I've been known to be wrong a time or two in my career." He was lying. If Darren's ever been wrong, it was way before I'd been teamed up with him. I prided myself on my methodical thinking and my honed skills as a detective, but while I was good, Darren was better.

"Then I guess I'll be sending her quarterly prison packages and be thankful that I'll pass the background for conjugal visits," I replied, shooting him a look.

Darren laughed. "Damn, Stud," he whistled. "Only one week, and you're already in love. She must be something else."

I sensed a dirty joke coming on, so I nixed it. "Don't, Dar."

He smiled as he shook his head. "I wasn't going to say anything, Stud," he denied. He let a heartbeat of silence go by before saying, "Just watch yourself, Theo. Even though Ridley and Horrace have the case now, you still gotta tell them anything you find out."

"I know," I assured him, and I *did* know. We may not be in charge of the case anymore, but we were still cops, and we still supported each other and treated everything like evidence.

When we passed the case over to Ridley and Horrace, we had turned over everything that we'd had on the case, including our gut instincts. We'd gone over Jeremiah Jackson's questioning-*a person that I still hadn't figured out his relationship with Callie*-Callie's questioning-*to where they had both laughed their asses off*-and Ryan Jones' questioning.

It'd been Ryan's brief interview that had caused the most concern for us all. How were you expected to narrow down a murderer when the victim was one of the most hated people in the city? Ryan had even been forthcoming about his own hate for the woman. It was basically a case of who *didn't* want to kill her.

Darren decided to stow away the big brother act. "C'mon," he said, jerking his head to the right. "Let's go see what this asshole has to tell us."

"It better be good," I told him. "If he got me out of Callie's bed to feed me some bullshit, I'm warning you now, I'm probably going to kick his ass."

Darren let out a low chuckle. "Fine by me," he said smoothly. "Besides, I'm sure that piece of shit has earned an ass whooping at some point in his life."

We entered the coffee giant, and Darren went to order us a couple of coffees while I headed towards the back table where Chaz sat, waiting on us.

"Hey, Chaz," I greeted as I sat down. "How's it going?"

Chaz eyed Darren as he made his way over to join us, two plain black coffees in hand. It was so early that the place was empty, so Darren got served quickly. It also didn't matter that we were in Starbucks, we drank our coffee straight.

I kept my eyes trained on Chaz and said, "This better be good, Chaz."

CHAPTER 21
Hot cop, indeed.

Callie ~

It was Sunday evening, and I was standing at Jeremiah's front door with Mexican take-out and a bottle of tequila. Tomorrow was going to be our first day back at the office after everything that happened, and I felt that Mexican food and liquor were appropriate fortification for the event.

Jeremiah's front door swung open, and his smile was like my happy place beacon. "Hey, babe," he greeted, stepping aside to let me in, then kissing the side of my head as I passed by.

I dropped the bag down on the kitchen island, then made myself at home, pulling down plates and glasses. Jeremiah opened the fridge, pulling out two Pepsis to go with dinner. The tequila was for dessert.

"Are you nervous?" I asked, getting straight to the point.

Jeremiah sat down on one of the stools as he set down the sodas. "You know, I don't know if I'm nervous, so much as anxious."

I plopped down on the bar stool next to him, then started opening up the bags of food. "Yeah," I muttered. "I know."

He shrugged a shoulder, but the movement was anything but casual. "It's…a bit disconcerting to imagine we might be working alongside a murderer."

I had a mouth full of chips and salsa when I blurted, "I'm sleeping with Detective Marsden."

The hand that was holding a tortilla chip full of salsaly goodness paused in midair, probably shocked by the change is subject. "Sleeping?" he asked. "As in *currently* sleeping with? Not *slept* with?"

I swallowed the mixture of Mexican heaven in my mouth before coming clean. "He came by after you left my place last week, and…he's sort of…been around for the past few days."

Jeremiah let out a harrumph. "I'm glad you gave him another chance, Cee Cee," he said, his voice genuine. "Still, it's not a conflict of interest?"

I shook my head. "No, I don't think so. He and his partner handed the case off to another pair of detectives."

"So, then…?"

"Ugh," I huffed dramatically, right before I pushed my plate away, dropping my head on the counter. "I like him, Jay," I confessed. "I really, really, *really* like him."

Jeremiah chuckled. "Oh, I see," he teased. "Hot Cop is putting it down in the bedroom."

Hot cop, indeed.

Theo's body was a work of art. He had the broad shoulders, chiseled chest, big arms, cut abs…hell, even his legs were muscular and sexy. Plus, his dick was world class. It made sense that a man that good-looking should possess a big dick.

Plus, *Holy Mary, Mother of God,* what he could do with that dick. Not to mention his mouth, his tongue, and his fingers. He was all brawn and raw power when he was slamming into me, and his apparent desperation to possess my body made me feel desirable.

That was probably the main reason that I hadn't said anything when I'd noticed Theo bringing toiletries and a change of clothes to keep at my place. He had casually commented that, in his line of work, it made sense for him to keep those things at my condo. Still, something told me it had nothing to do with his job.

Or maybe it was just wishful thinking on my part.

Maybe I was just hoping that the intention meant more.

I raised my head as I pulled back my plate of Mexican yumminess. "It's not just the bedroom," I mumbled.

Jay let out a laugh. "Enjoy it, Callie. We're going to possibly be caught up in a murder investigation for a while," he pointed out. "You might as well get your joy where you can."

"He asked about you," I told him.

Jay laughed again. "I'd be disappointed in him if he hadn't," he chuckled. "What did you tell him?"

This time, I was the one that shrugged a shoulder. "I told him you were my best friend off hours and my partner in crime during work hours." I was never going to forget the look on Theo's face when I'd said that. "Admittedly, my choice in wording wasn't the best," I stated ruefully. "However, once I assured the detective in him that I hadn't meant that literally, he calmed down and didn't comment other than to *instruct* me to make it clear to you that he and I were an item."

Jay was all smiles. "I'm liking him better and better."

I rolled my eyes. "What is it with men and their caveman ways?"

He snorted. "If you ever meet a man that doesn't want to piss a ring around you, run away," Jay retorted. "He's either gay, and not really interested in you, or he's a pussy."

"That is not true," I argued. "Some guys just have sensitive souls."

"A sensitive soul has nothing to do with the size of your balls, Callie," he replied.

I wasn't going to get pulled into a debate with him about the battle of the sexes. It was an argument that would never, ever be solved. Besides, I secretly liked that Theo had been a little jealous.

I cut off that conversation and asked, "Who do you think did it, Jay?"

He let out a deep breath. "Even though my first choice is still Ryan, I've thought about it almost all week, Cee Cee. It could be anybody-*literally.*" He was right. I'd just been hoping that he might have had some insight that I might have missed. "She was a horrible, horrible, different type of evil. Who *didn't* want to see her dead?"

I nodded. "Do you remember when Ashley, the front desk receptionist, was going through a divorce and Margot told her if she caught her crying one more time that she'd suspend her for lowering morale in the workplace?"

Jeremiah visibly winced. "Do you remember the time Ryan's father passed away and Margot asked him if he really wanted to waste his bereavement leave on a man who was a cheating asshole?"

I was certain that I'd never forget that day. We'd been in the middle of a staff meeting when she had asked Ryan that offensive and cruel question, and how she knew anything about Ryan's father, I had no idea.

"How about when she walked in on Cody telling us about the girl that he'd met, and Margot told him to just give up on women because women weren't attracted to pussies with small dicks."

"Jesus Christ," he muttered. "How about the time that Margot told Carmen that she was turning kissing ass into an Olympic sport."

I cringed at the memories. "Remember when she told Brent that we could wait until he was done trying to get into Lucia's pants to finish our staff meeting?"

Jeremiah shook his head, grunting. "Fuck, Callie. The real mystery isn't who killed her, but that it took this long for someone to finally off her."

We sat there in silence-well, except for the crunch of the tortilla chips-letting our minds wander over the millions of possibilities, and I wasn't exaggerating with the million count. I couldn't imagine anyone who's ever met Margot not wanting to kill her.

Then a thought crossed my mind that I wished I could unthink. "Oh, God, Jay," I muttered. "I wonder how many men she had to extort, pay, or threaten to sleep with her. I mean, how can any man stand to be in her company long enough to stick it to her?"

Jeremiah groaned and it wasn't in a sexy way, either. "Don't make me throw up all this delicious food, Callie. Talk about traumatizing the mind."

Curiosity had me wanting to ask Theo what was going on, but I didn't want to put him in an awkward position. I had to trust that he'd tell me anything that would affect me personally, and he had to trust that I hadn't killed Margot.

A relationship made in paradise, for sure.

Jay must have been reading my mind because he turned and cocked his head, regarding me closely. "How does Theo feel about you going back to work with a possible murderer?"

I brought my shoulders up in a shrug. "I don't know," I admitted. "We don't talk about the case."

His brows rose. "Like, at all?"

I shook my head. "At all," I confirmed. "I'm not sure if it's because he doesn't know or if he doesn't trust me."

Jay wrapped an arm around my shoulders. "Maybe it's neither, Callie," he said soothingly. "Maybe he's just trying to protect you and what you guys have."

Maybe. However, I wasn't so sure. "Well, to be fair, we don't do much talking when he's around," I said wryly.

One brow arched. "Meaning?"

I could hear the disapproval in his voice. "Not like that, Jay," I quickly corrected. "He's just gone so much." I shrugged again. "When he does come around, we spend our time together or sleeping."

"So, there *are* times he goes over, crawls in your bed, and just holds you?" he asked.

I knew that he was just trying to protect me from being just a piece of ass. I leaned over, nudging his shoulder. "Yeah, there is." I said, hoping to calm him. "Sometimes we have sex, sometimes we just sleep, and sometimes we fall asleep on the couch."

He gave me one terse nod. "As long as he's not using you, he's got my vote."

I gave him my most outraged expression. "Hey! How do you know I'm not using *him?*"

He laughed. "Because you're not made that way, Cee Cee."

"I could be," I argued.

"Nah, girl," he countered. "That's one thing you'd never be."

CHAPTER 22
You got me?

Theo ~

I was updating a report when Spencer Ridley leaned up against my desk. I stopped typing, then looked up at him. "What's up?"

"Calvin and I spent all week interviewing everyone who worked in that goddamn building, and I gotta say-" He shook his head. "-the stories have been incredible."

I nodded. "Yeah," I agreed. "Just from the little that Darren and I had touched on, the vic seemed like a real piece of work."

His eyes started darting around, then he reached down and began fiddling with the papers in my folder tray. I gave him a moment before he finally returned his blue gaze back to mine. "See, the thing is…"

"What? Just fucking say it," I instructed, hoping it would prompt him to spit out whatever he was trying to say. He wasn't one of my favorite people, though we got along well enough.

"Everyone's been pretty forthcoming with their stories, and most of them have even been eager to share their tales of horror," he said. "All employees, except for two." My jaw clenched. I knew what he was going to say before he said it. "A Mr. Jeremiah Jackson and a Ms. Callie Callows."

I knew where he was going with this, and I wasn't about to let him. I had serious issues about this case; mainly, the fact that Callie could possibly be working side by side with a murderer. Her safety was what mattered most to me. However, knowing what I knew about Margot Livingston, and with everything Spencer just told me, I didn't think we were dealing with an outright killer. Margot Livingston was rotten to the core, and it appeared as if someone just couldn't take her abuse anymore.

It was almost akin to battered woman syndrome. The person that she'd been abusing just couldn't take another round of abuse from the woman. However, it wasn't unheard of for someone who's killed to get a taste for it. So, my concern for Callie was still very real and still very warranted.

"Yeah, Darren and I met up with that same roadblock during the initial interviewing," I admitted, though he already knew that. We'd told him during our pass down.

Ridley arched a dark blonde brow. "So, you're telling me that Ms. Callows lawyered up, even though you're fucking her? Do you suck in the sack or something, Marsden?"

I stood up, and while he straightened to his full height, he still had to look up at me. "Watch yourself, Ridley," I warned. "You can speculate on my dick all you want. Hell, I'll even let you keep dreaming about it and wondering how good in bed I really am." Stepping into his space, I added, "But you will watch how you speak about Callie because what I'm not doing is *fucking* her. You got me?"

He threw his hands up in mock surrender. "Hey, relax, man," he said. "I'm just saying, you know how we cops feel about people who don't cooperate willingly. Just makes you wonder what they might be hiding, is all."

"Callie isn't hiding anything," I insisted. "She's just doing what everyone should do when questioned by the cops, and that's protect themselves from confusion."

"The pussy must be really good if she's making you forget which side of the law you're on," he sneered. My arm was already cocked back as Darren and Horrace jumped in between us. We hadn't exactly kept our voices down.

"Hey, hey, hey," Darren chimed in, his hands patting my chest as I watched Horrace push Ridley back. "We're all on the same team, remember?"

"Oh, yeah?" Spencer spat. "Well, remind your partner of that and get him to get his girlfriend to fucking talk to us."

"Fuck you, Ridley," I fired back. "You know just as well as I do that I need to stay the fuck out of this case."

"That doesn't mean you can't convince her to talk to us," he challenged. "Or maybe you just don't want to admit that she might be hiding something. Her and her little BFF, Jeremiah Jackson." Then, just to piss me off more, he added, "Not a bad-looking guy is he, Marsden?"

I huffed out a humorless laugh. "Why don't you suck my dick, Ridley?"

"Okay, okay. Enough!" Horrace shouted before turning to me. "Ridley's an asshole, I get it," he conceded. "But he's right, Theo. You need to get your girlfriend and her friend to talk to us. By the looks of it, it appears that the entire world hated Ms. Livingston, and since your girlfriend works in the H.R. Department, her questioning is critical, and you know it."

I *did* know it.

Callie being the H.R. Manager made her privy to all sorts of complaints and possible motives. In all honesty, I was pretty certain that my relationship with her was the only reason that Ridley and Horrace hadn't gone after her as aggressively as they normally would have with an uncooperative witness.

I'd never been so torn before and it fucking sucked.

I was a cop. It was all that I'd ever wanted to be, and I was good at it. As a cop, I should be urging Callie and Jeremiah to cooperate in the investigation. As a cop, I should be reassuring Callie that she was safe and that an interview was just that-an interview. No one was trying to trip her up or accuse her of anything.

I also understood her reluctancy.

I really did.

As much as it pained me to admit, there *were* bad cops out there. There were innocent people that *had been* railroaded when they'd found themselves dealing with crooked law enforcement. There were cops that *did* turn interviews into bullying sessions. So, I didn't blame someone if they asked for a lawyer. I didn't blame people if they were leery about speaking to law enforcement. However, Callie's absolute refusal was a bit extreme. I mean, how could she not know that I'd never let anything happen to her?

Plus, she didn't have a history of run-ins with the law or a childhood full of negative experiences with cops. Or, at least, that I knew of. In all honesty, while we talked, we still had a lot to learn about each other. I wasn't exactly in a rush to extract every detail of the life that she'd lived. I was serious about Callie, so we had plenty of time to learn about each other's childhoods and the like.

It was just, right now, the man in me wanted to spend as much time as I could inside her, so that she wouldn't come to resent my sporadic schedule and long hours. I figured if I continuously fucked her into oblivion, then she'd convince herself I was worth the headache.

I did my best to calm down and start thinking like a cop, instead of a protective boyfriend. "I'll talk to her," I acquiesced, feeling like I was somehow betraying Callie. Maybe not *actually* betraying, but definitely not respecting her wishes.

Ridley let out an exaggerated sigh. "See?" he said. "That's all I was fucking asking for."

"Well, your delivery needs some fucking work," I snapped back. "And if you ever speak about Callie in a disrespectful manner again, I will fuck you up, Ridley." He flipped me the bird as Horrace helped escort him away.

The crowd dispersed, and everyone went back to work. Darren waited until all eyes were elsewhere before he spoke. "Ridley's a dick."

I dropped back into my seat as I looked up at Darren. "But?"

"But he's not wrong, Stud," he replied. "Callie's their best chance at narrowing down who truly hated the victim at work and who was just an average disgruntled employee. Plus, with that friend of hers also not talking, it could just be a simple case of her trying to protect him."

"You think it was Jeremiah Jackson?" I hadn't really given him any thought. Hell, since the case had been taken away from us, I hadn't really given any of it any real thought. My sole focus had been Callie and it still was.

"I don't know, man," he said. "Now that it's not our case, I don't know enough to have an opinion on the guy one way or another." He shrugged his shoulder. "But I do know Callie's the difference between them wrapping up the case and it dragging the hell on."

I closed my eyes as I dropped my head in my hands. He was right. They were all right. I just didn't want to push her. I also sure as fuck didn't want her thinking that I was only sleeping with her as a way to get her to cooperate, either.

I'd lose her for sure.

I ran my hands down my face, then looked up at my partner. "I know, Dar. I know, and I'm going to talk to her about it."

"Be sure that you do," he encouraged. "If Horrace and Ridley have to resort to dragging her in here, it's not going to go well. Not to mention, it'll put you in an awfully uncomfortable position."

I watched as he walked away, then turning in my chair, I stared down at the papers on my desk, not really seeing anything. Taking me off this case was supposed to eliminate any possible drama like this.

What the fuck?

Still, one thing that I did know was that I'd gotten addicted to Callie rather quickly, and I was not about to let this shit come between us.

I didn't know why she was so against speaking with the police because I was apprehensive about bringing up the subject to her. I trusted my attraction to her, and having never felt like this about anyone before, I wasn't eager to rock the boat just yet.

Hell, she'd had no issue with telling me to go fuck myself while being questioned about a goddamn murder. I had no doubt that she'd tell me to kick rocks if I pushed her too hard on this.

Maybe after we've been married a couple of years, and she was pregnant with my child, I might feel secure enough to ask her why she hated the police.

CHAPTER 23
Thank God.

Callie ~
"Oh, God…"

"I could fuck you every hour, and I still wouldn't get tired of this tight pussy, baby," Theo panted between thrusts, and I couldn't agree more.

Everything about Theo was addicting, but the way that the man fucked was beyond spectacular. I couldn't get enough of him, and I didn't care how much sleep it cost me. I would gladly give up rest and food to be with him.

"Yes…" I whimpered. "Please, Theo…"

"God, I love it when you beg for my cock," he grunted above me.

Missionary had been given a bad rap about being boring, but it was my favorite position. I loved being caged in by a man's superior size and strength. It made me feel sheltered and protected at the same time that I was being used for his pleasure. It was a perfect exchange of power.

It wasn't long before my body was falling over, tremors of ecstasy wracking my entire being. I came all over his cock, and he fucked me through my orgasm until he was spilling himself inside me.

That was the best part.

I'd never had sex without a condom before Theo, but there was something to be said for how intimate that dirty act was. I loved being covered in him, even if that made me a hoebag.

Tonight, we were at Theo's house, and he'd been trying to convince me to move some of my stuff over, kind of like the stuff that he had at my house. I had argued that it wasn't necessary since we spent most of our time at my place, but I could tell that it had bothered him a bit. However, I didn't think that I was being difficult; I was just being practical.

I curled into his body, and as he wrapped his arm around me, I told him, "I love how you make my body feel."

He chuckled. "Oh, really? And how do I make your body feel?"

I sighed contently. "Like I never want to come out from under you," I confessed. "Ever." Theo's arm tightened around me while his other arm reached over, pulling my leg over his waist, and that's all I remembered before falling into a deep slumber.

I wasn't sure how long I'd slept for, but I knew that I was screwed when Theo's absence in bed was the thing that had woken me up. However, I chalked it up to not being completely comfortable in his bed yet. Whenever we were at my house, I had no problem sleeping through his ins and outs of my bed, and thank God for that, or else I'd never get any sleep.

I climbed out of bed, then reached for my clothes. I didn't have anything to sleep in over here, so I usually just threw on one of Theo's shirts. However, I couldn't find his discarded shirt anywhere on the floor. After throwing on my panties and t-shirt, I made my way to find him when I was stopped short in the hallway by a voice that wasn't Theo's.

"Yeah, so now that Chaz is dead, we're in this bullshit deeper."

"Jesus," Theo replied. "I thought the motherfucker was being smart about his shit."

"Yeah, well, apparently not," the other voice said, one I finally recognized. The voice belonged to his partner, Detective Franklin.

I didn't want to intrude on what was obviously work, so I decided to head back into the bedroom. However, that plan changed when Detective Franklin spoke again. "And what about Callie?"

"I think Chaz turning up dead takes a little more precedence over Callie, don't you think, Dar?" came Theo's reply. "I mean, our case is the Magdallini murder, not the Livingston murder."

"Yeah, and I'm not confused about that, Stud," Detective Franklin responded. "But you did say you were going to get Callie to talk, and it's been a couple of days already. Any progress?"

My heart dropped into that hollow pit at the bottom of my stomach.

What was he talking about?

"I haven't had a chance to really bring it up," Theo answered.

I could hear Detective Franklin let out an incredulous laugh. "Oh, c'mon, Theo," he chided. "You've been sleeping with her damn near every night for a couple of weeks now. Are you seriously telling me that you still haven't gotten any pillow talk out of it?"

I threw my hands over my mouth to muffle my gasp.

Oh, my God.

Theo's been sleeping with me just to try to find out what I knew about Margot's murder???

Hurt and humiliation skittered throughout my body. All that talk about how we shared this special feeling between just the two of us had been bullshit. All that insistence about how I hadn't needed to be embarrassed about the things that I let him do to me had been a lie.

God, how could I be such a fool?

I didn't wait to hear Theo's response. I ran back to the room, then threw on my pants, bra, socks, and shoes in record time. I wanted to cry. I wanted to fall to the ground, curl up into a fetal position, then cry until the pain subsided. However, pride had me by my ear, twisting it, and it was telling me to get my shit together and wait to fall apart at home.

I glanced around Theo's bedroom, then gave myself a mental high five that there wasn't anything else that I needed to grab other than my purse. All this time, something had been preventing me from bringing my stuff over and getting comfortable, and I thanked God for it now. If I knew what that something was, I'd take it to dinner and buy it diamonds, because finding out that Theo was only using me to solve a case, that something was going to help me keep my humiliating exit to a minimum.

I counted to ten, and by the grace of God, I put one foot in front of the other as I straightened my backbone, then walked out of Theo's bedroom, down the hallway, and into the living room where both men stood.

Detective Franklin was dressed in his custom detective gear of tan slacks, a light blue button up, and a dark brown jacket. I presumed the jacket was used more as a concealer for his gun than anything to actually keep warm with.

In contrast, Theo was barefoot and in a pair of jeans and the t-shirt I had pulled off his body earlier. He looked exactly like a man who'd gotten called out of bed.

My eyes darted over towards the couch, and I could see the straps of my purse hanging over the side of the armrest of the couch.

Thank God.

I stalked over to the couch, then grabbed my purse, ignoring both men.

It wasn't until I had my purse in my hands that Theo spoke. "What are you doing?" His voice, sounding so genuine in surprise, nearly did me in.

I looked over at him, then prayed that I had the strength to get through this without humiliating myself any more than I already felt. "I'm leaving," I answered flatly.

He glanced over at Detective Franklin, and then turned those chocolate browns back towards me. "Darren was just-"

"I know what Detective Franklin was just doing," I interrupted. "He's here, checking on your progress, right, Detective Marsden?" Theo flinched, and that's when I knew that I had him. More importantly, he knew it, too. I looked over at Detective Franklin and said, "Sorry if I ruined your plans to crack Margot's case, Detective Franklin, but all Detective Marsden has been able to find out is just how rough I like my sex."

"Callie!"

"Ms. Cal-"

I let out a humorous laugh, shutting them both up. "You guys wondered why I wouldn't talk without a lawyer. Well-" I threw my right hand up and gestured towards the both of them. "-this, right here, is why," I explained. "While most cops are good and decent, you still have the few that fall through the cracks, and those are the ones that the public needs to protect themselves against." I let out another awful laugh. "And it looks like I was right to not cooperate, because the two cops that *I* got came with no shame about fucking a witness for information."

Theo took a step towards me. "Callie, that's not-"

"Take one more step, Detective, and I will be in front of a news camera first thing in the morning, telling the whole world how our wonderful, respected, *professional* police force likes to investigate its cases," I threatened, praying that he'd stay where he was. I was playing a great hand of poker right now, but I didn't think that I'd be able to keep it up if he touched me.

He stayed where he was, but he kept talking. "Callie, please listen to me," he pleaded. "It's not what you think-"

"God, you must think me twenty times an idiot to tell me it's not what I think when I heard you guys talking loud, clear, and in perfectly good English." I said, stepping towards the front door.

I had the front door open when Theo tried again. *"Callie, fucking listen to me-"*

"Don't think so, Detective," I scoffed before looking back at him and his partner, and fuck an arrest record, I told them exactly what I thought of them both. "You guys are worse than the criminals you arrest," I spat. "At least the criminals aren't trying to pretend that they're good when they're not."

I slammed the door behind me, then ran down Theo's walkway onto the sidewalk and around the block. The irony wasn't lost on me, either. This was the same route that I'd taken when I had executed my morning-after walk of shame the morning after we'd met.

Only it was more than shame this time around.

It was humiliation at its most painful.

CHAPTER 24

Hell, I still might.

Theo ~

I sat at my desk, hoping that the stacks of paperwork would do me a solid and occupy my mind, but so far, it wasn't working.

After Callie had run out on me yesterday, I had spent hours calling her, texting her, and leaving countless voicemails. Eventually the calls had bounced back, and I knew that she had finally blocked me.

Darren had told me to give her a couple of days to cool down, but I thought that was a horrible plan. In my opinion, the worst thing that a man could do was give a woman time to realize that she'd be just fine without him. The only reason that I hadn't broken down her front door was because I didn't want to lose my career over stalking and harassment charges.

There was also the fact that, no matter how many times I fucking tried, I couldn't erase that look on her face from my mind. It had been a look of utter betrayal, and it was slowly eating me alive. It was all that I could think about.

I had always been proud to be a cop. I took pride in every aspect of the job. I had advanced quickly, and it had been all due to hard fucking work. However, her quick accusation, lumping me in with dirty cops, had cut me to the quick. I *despised* dirty cops. They were worse than the criminals that we chased because-like Callie had so ruthlessly pointed out-at least we knew that we couldn't trust the criminals. At least we knew what we were dealing with when chasing the bad guys.

However, dirty cops? Men who had sworn to uphold the law and protect the city's citizens, only to get into bed with the people they were supposed to be taking down? Well, they really were the dredges of the scum-ridden streets.

Callie believed me to be the type of cop-the type of *man*-that would use sex as an interrogation tool, and I was finding that difficult to absorb.

"Theo?"

I had no idea how I was going to make this better, but I knew there was no way that I was going to be able to let Callie go. Even if she didn't believe it right now, I'd meant everything that I'd said to her. I believed with every fiber of my being that the feelings we shared were rare.

"Theo!"

My head snapped up, and I looked over my desk and across Darren's to see him staring at me with frustration written all over his face. "What?"

Darren let out a sigh. "I said that I just got a tip to talk to a Flip Castle pertaining to Chaz," he answered.

My brows furrowed. *"Flip Castle?"* I asked. "Is that the dude's real name?"

Darren's brows rose. "Yep," he said. "I looked it up, and the man has a rap sheet claiming that is his real name."

I let out a deep breath, stood up, then grabbing my jacket from my chair, said, "Well, then, let's go talk to Flip."

"Hey, Marsden?"

I turned towards the sound of my name, and I saw Ridley walking towards me. "Ah, fuck." I heard Darren mumble as I crossed my arms over my chest, waiting for Ridley to approach. I didn't blame Darren. With how fucked-up I was over Callie, it wouldn't take much for me to knock this motherfucker out.

"You guys heading out?" he asked as he took in Darren putting on his jacket.

"Yeah," I clipped out. "We just got a tip on one of our murders, so what do you want?"

The corner of his lip curled in a smirk that I wanted to knock off his face. "I just wanted to say thank you, man."

Everything in me screamed to just walk away from this asshole, but the cop's curiosity in me couldn't. "Thanks for what?"

"Horrace and I just got a call from a couple of Melko lawyers, along with Dean and Bianca Milton, scheduling an appointment later today for the questioning of a Mr. Jeremiah Jackson and Ms. Callie Callows," he informed me, all shark tooth smiles.

I did my best not to give myself away, but his news was like a boot to the kidney. Callie was finally cooperating, and my gut was telling me that it was so that she could be done with the entire case, the entire police department, and me.

"Hope their interviews help," I replied honestly.

"I guess I can't talk shit about you being a bust in the sack anymore if you were able to get her to come in," he ribbed.

Darren must have ESP because he was in between us before I could take a step. "Enough, Ridley," he barked. "Handle your shit and leave us to handle ours. We've got shit to do."

Ridley stepped back with his hands up in mock surrender. "Hey," he chuckled. "I was just saying thanks, man."

I walked past him, not trusting myself to speak, and Darren followed. God, I wanted to punch that motherfucker out.

Hell, I still might.

Darren and I were riding the elevator down when he said, "Look, man, I know you're upset and this entire thing is a shitshow right now, but you can't go around knocking assholes out, no matter how much they might deserve it."

I ran my hands through my hair. "I know, Dar," I huffed. "And I'm not going to fuck him up, I promise. I'm just…today's not the day, ya know."

He sighed. I noticed that he'd been doing a lot of that lately. "I know, Stud. I know," he said. "I just don't want you letting one heated moment ruin the rest of your life."

"I'm not going to ruin anything, Darren," I assured him. "I just need to figure out what I'm going to do about Callie. I'm telling you, giving her space was the wrong thing to do."

Darren chuckled. "It's never a good thing to tangle with a pissed off woman, Stud."

"Better a pissed off woman in the heat of the moment, than an indifferent one a few days later," I retorted. I shook my head. "She already didn't like cops or cared for one-night stands, Dar. Everything I am, or have been, is a point against me."

The elevator came to a stop at the precinct's lobby, and once the doors slid open, we walked out. Heading out the side door, Darren finally commented on my statement. "The thing is, when you're with her, you're not a cop or a one-night stand; you've just been Theo. I think once she calms down, she'll see those accusations were uncalled for."

We made our way to the car in silence, partly because I didn't believe him, but mostly because speculation wasn't going to help me.

When Callie had threatened me with media coverage if I'd taken one more step towards her, I had *believed* her. There'd been no doubt in my mind that she would have followed through with her threat, and because I could feel her conviction from across the fucking living room, I knew that it was going to be an uphill battle to regain her trust.

The biggest problem with strong women was that they were very aware that they didn't need a man to survive. They didn't need one to succeed or be happy. Hell, in this day and age, they didn't even need one to start a family. They could adopt or go the clinical route.

Strong women were with you because they *wanted* to be with you, not because they *needed* to be with you. Now, while it would normally make a man feel like a king because he'd been chosen out of emotion instead of necessity, the drawback was that a strong woman had no qualms about walking away if you hurt her. Plus, even though I was pretty positive that I'd been giving Callie the best sex of her life, I doubted that'd be enough for her to just forgive my carelessness.

There was also the fact that she was probably going to work every day with a murderer. As much as I wanted to bug the shit out of Ridley and Horrace for details about the case, I'd done my best to concentrate on my case load and stay out of it. Still, it's been a struggle.

I unlocked the car, and as I sat behind the steering wheel, Darren looked over at me and drawled out dramatically, "Are you sure you're okay to drive, Stud?" I cocked my head at him. "I'm just saying," he chuckled. "I don't want you wrapping us around a telephone pole because you're distraught over your woman troubles." I flipped him off, then turned the ignition.

I pulled out of the parking lot and onto the street, still wondering what the fuck I was going to do in order to convince Callie that she misunderstood what she'd overheard. Maybe I'd get just an unpaid suspended leave of absence if I got arrested for stalking and harassment. I mean, it was possible...

"Quit thinking so hard," Darren said, snapping me back to reality. "Get your head in the game. Callie's not going anywhere."

I didn't bother looking at him when I asked, "How do you know she's not?"

"Because no woman gets that pissed off unless she cares, Stud," he stated, oh, so wisely. "That should give you an in at another chance."

I decided not to comment. There was no point. It didn't matter if a man grew up with seventeen sisters; no man would ever be able to understand the mind of a woman, and therein laid the challenge as old as time.

CHAPTER 25
Fuck you, very much, Detective Ridley.

Callie ~

I resented having to be here.

I resented caving.

I also sure as hell resented that whoever offed Margot had done it on company property, which led to me having to be here. Why couldn't they have killed her at her home? It was goddamn inconsiderate if you asked me. I mean, seriously.

I stood inside the city's sleek-looking police station with Jeremiah on one side and Bianca Milton on the other. Next to her, stood Gary Hertz, and on the other side of Jeremiah, stood Dean Milton and Candice Moray.

Gary Hertz and Candice Moray were two of Melko's corporate lawyers. Dean and Bianca Milton were a married team of criminal defense lawyers, and they were reputed to be smarter than Einstein and more lethal than a Great White shark.

After I'd left Theo's the other night, I had run straight to Jay's and had cried out the entire sordid story. It had taken a good two hours to finally calm me down, and I'd been so exhausted from the cryfest that I had crashed where I laid, and that had been on his couch.

The next morning, I had ended up telling Jeremiah that I wanted to give my interview in hopes that, if I did, the police would be done with me, and I'd never have to have anything to do with them anymore. Jeremiah had immediately known that I'd meant having anything to do with Theo, but he hadn't called me out on it. Instead, we had contacted Corporate H.R. as soon as we'd gotten to work. A lot of corporate figures were still on the premises, considering Margot's killer hadn't been caught yet, so it'd been easy to get corporate representation.

They also believed that since me and Jeremiah had been holding out, it was best to have corporate representation to stave off any liability comments and criminal representation to stave off any accidental incrimination. I had to admit, when they'd told me they had secured Dean and Bianca Milton, I'd been super impressed.

As soon as we walked in, all eyes fell on us, but I knew it was because Dean and Bianca had entered the building and their strides were bold, confident, and intimidating. When we reached the front desk, Dean informed the welcoming officer that we were here to meet with Detectives Spencer Ridley and Colin Horrace. After a few ticks on her computer, we were given visitor badges and instructed to use the elevator to the third floor. She had already called ahead, so Detective Ridley and Detective Horrace should be there to greet us.

I was starting to loath the word 'detective'.

We all entered the elevator, and Jeremiah grabbed hold of my hand and squeezed. However, instead of letting go, he held on, then laced his fingers through mine. Now, everyone else might think that it was a sweet gesture between a nervous couple, but it wasn't. Jeremiah knew there was a chance that we'd see Theo here somewhere and this was his quiet way of trying to show me some support.

Thank God, too, because I needed it.

Once the elevator doors opened, the men stepped back, allowing me, Candice, and Bianca to exit first, and then they trailed behind us like gentlemen. Jeremiah grabbed my hand again as we were approached by two men.

The blonde one looked to be six-foot and fit. He was kind of plain-looking, but not unattractive. The redhead walking next to him looked to be the same height and slim. I wasn't a fan of Gingers, but the man was actually good-looking. It worked for him.

The blonde stuck out his hand as he approached, and the first person that his hand went to for introductions was me. "Ms. Callows, I'm Detective Spencer Ridley and this is my partner, Detective Colin Horrace." I placed my free hand in his. "Thank you so much for coming in." I didn't comment as he moved the introductions onto Jeremiah, Gary, and Candice. Once he got to Dean, he said, "Dean, good to see you again."

Dean Milton laughed. "Cut the shit, Ridley," he smirked. "Neither of you are happy to see me or Bianca." I looked over at them, and Bianca had a stunning smile plastered across her face at what her husband just said. "Let's just get this over with, so my clients can move on with their lives, yeah?"

Detective Horrace smiled back. "Time is money after all, right, Milton?" He didn't wait for Dean to comment, but continued, "So, what are the teams?"

"Dean and Mrs. Moray will accompany Mr. Jackson, and Mr. Hertz and I will accompany Ms. Callows," Bianca Milton answered, finally speaking.

"Great," Detective Ridley replied. "I'll take Ms. Callows and Detective Horrace will take Mr. Jackson, if that's good with everyone."

Dean rolled his eyes. "C'mon, let's get this show on the road."

Detective Horrace stretched his arm out, indicating the direction we were to go, but before we started walking, Jeremiah wrapped me in his arms and whispered in my ear, "It's going to be fine Cee Cee." I gave him a quick nod before following the detectives.

When we got to a hallway comprised of doors on each side, Detective Ridley opened one of the doors on the right and ushered me, Bianca, and Gary inside while his partner opened a door on the opposite side, ushering in Jay, Dean, and Candice.

We all sat, Bianca and Gary on either side of me, and Detective Ridley sitting across the table in front of me. The interrogation room looked exactly like it did in the movies.

"Would you like anything to drink, Ms. Callows?" I was about to politely decline when his next words had me wanting to walk out the door. "I don't want it getting back to Detective Marsden that you weren't treated well." He winked at me, and I wanted to gouge his eyeballs out.

A little extreme? Maybe. However, the man came off like a douche.

Instead of commenting, I looked over at Gary, then said, "Why don't you just give him the diary, Mr. Hertz."

He nodded, then pulling out a thick notebook from his brown briefcase, he tossed it on the table towards Detective Ridley. "That, there, is an unofficial account of all of Ms. Livingston's less-than-professional…uh, incidents as logged by Ms. Callows."

Detective Ridley's brows rose as his hands reached for the diary. We sat quietly as he skimmed through some of the pages. The expressions that ran across his face were sure indicators of shock and disgust.

When he finally looked up at me, he asked, "Why are these complaints unofficial, Ms. Callows? I mean, by your own accounts, she seemed like a monster."

"After you read it in detail, you'll see that none of those incidents were actually directly related to me," I explained. "They were incidences that I witnessed, but because everyone was so afraid of losing their jobs, no formal complaints were ever made against her."

He sat up straighter. "Why didn't you file one as the H.R. Manager?"

Even if he wasn't, I felt like he was judging me. "Because without corroborating witnesses and accounts, it would be my word against hers, and I wasn't about to throw myself on the sword for anyone not willing to back me up." I raised a brow at his maybe-maybe not-judgey ways. "I have bills to pay, too, Detective."

He nodded. "Fair enough," he replied simply. "So, then how about you tell me why you refused to speak to us until now?"

I looked over at Bianca, and she gave me a slight nod of her head. "Murder is a serious thing, Detective Ridley. I didn't feel comfortable giving my opinions of others that might…uh, skew how you saw them or interviewed them. Because that's all they would be, *my opinions.*"

He leaned forward on the desk, then clasped his hands together in front of him. "So, if I was to ask you, based on all the things you've witnessed, who you thought it could be, you're answer would be…?"

I mimicked his posture before saying, "No one, everyone, and anyone, Detective. She was a hateful person, and her hateful personality was not limited to within the walls of Melko. She was mean to everyone she ever came in contact with." I looked him square in the eye when I delivered my final statement. "Do your own legwork, Detective, because I have nothing for you other than that diary."

"Do you honestly think we're done here, Ms. Callows?" he asked, trying to give off the illusion of control.

Before I could answer, Bianca Milton smirked. "We *are* done, Detective," she announced. "You have the cooperation of Melko by evidence of the diary, and you have Ms. Callows' statement as to why she was hesitant for an interview. You also have her interview now, which suggests she doesn't know anything further."

"What are you talking about?" he snapped back. "I haven't even asked her any real questions yet. I haven't established her alibi, *her* relationship with the deceased, or anything of real substance."

Bianca looked over at me, and this time, it was me giving her the slight nod. "You have fifteen minutes to ask all the questions you need to," Bianca informed him. "But make them count, Detective, because we *will* be out of here in fifteen minutes."

Mr. Hertz chimed in before Detective Ridley could begin his questioning, "And please limit those questions to the relevance of Ms. Livingston's murder, Detective. The company has already cooperated, and if you need to know anything else, company related, it's not going to come from Ms. Callows."

I looked across the table at Detective Ridley's red face, and I couldn't stop the smile that took over my entire expression.

Fuck you, very much, Detective Ridley.

CHAPTER 26
Fuck it.

Theo ~

I knocked on the door and wondered for the millionth time if Callie was going to answer it, let alone let me into her condo.

I hadn't been back at the station for more than twenty minutes when Ridley had approached me and had given me the run down on how he had questioned Callie and Jeremiah that morning. He hadn't given me details, but he had informed me that Callie and Jeremiah had both been accompanied by a few sharks.

The surprise visit had me hoping that Callie might be more open to speaking to me with the questioning now out of the way. Hence, me standing in front of the door to her condo.

I knocked again and heard a muffled *'coming'* from the other side of the door. No lie…a part of me actually considered moving to the side, out of the way of the peephole, so that she couldn't see that it was me. However, I quickly remembered that I wasn't ten-years-old anymore.

I stood firm, and when the door swung open, it was all I could do from taking her in my arms and marching us towards her bedroom. She was dressed in a pair of tiny, pink, loose running shorts and a form-fitting, white, no-good-excuse for a tank top. Her tits were on grand display, and I didn't know if I'd have the ability to hold a conversation with her, let alone apologize. Her hair was thrown up in a messy bun and her feet were barefoot. My guess was that she must be cleaning her condo.

"What are you doing here?" she asked in a voice that was so emotionless that I actually would prefer it if she were screeching like a banshee.

"May I come in?"

Please, let me come in, baby.

"For what?" she asked, her face as emotionless as her voice.

"C'mon, Callie," I said, softening my voice. "I'd like to talk."

She arched a brow. "Just talk?" she smirked. "What? You're not interested in fucking me now that I've given my interview?"

All plans of being a nice guy flew out the window at the reminder of what she thought of me as a cop-as a *man*. I used my height and size to muscle her backwards until I was slamming her front door shut with one hand and pushing her up against the wall with the other. Her green crystals widened, but she didn't back down or struggle to free herself.

I had one hand around her throat and the other flat against the wall when I leaned down-making sure that her green gaze was focused on my brown one-and said, "Don't ever think that I don't want to spend every second of my days and nights balls-deep inside your hot, wet, little cunt, Callie. I *dream* of it. I fucking *fantasize* about it all day at work," I hissed. "I sit at my goddamn desk and replay images in my head of all the times that I've seen your perfect fucking face covered in my cum. I fight erections all damn day, remembering how tight your ass feels wrapped around my cock."

Fuck it.

While I kept her in place with my right hand still circling her throat, I slid my other hand down past her shoulder, over her tit, then across her stomach until it was palming her tight, moist, hot pussy. Her breath hitched as I immediately slid two fingers inside her heat and pressed my palm against her clit.

Her hands grabbed my wrist and forearm, but she didn't push me away or pull my hand out of her panties. I didn't stop talking as I finger fucked the hell out of her, either. "There's not an hour of my day that goes by where I don't picture you with your ankles around your ears, giving me a perfect view of your addicting fuckholes, Callie." She let out a low moan and actually started grinding against my hand, and if I had to slut talk her into an orgasm to make her forgive me, then I was all about it. Anything to make her forgive me.

Any-fucking-thing.

I leaned down farther until my lips were next to her ear. "Don't tell me you don't miss my cock in your pussy, baby. Because I know *I* miss it," I growled. "I miss hearing your soft cries because it hurts at first. I miss how, even though it hurts, you still let me slide my cock deep inside you because you're so turned on that you can't tell me no."

"Theo..." she whimpered as she started really riding my hand.

"But you want to know what I miss the most, Callie?" I didn't wait for or expect an answer. "I miss your voice begging me to cum inside your pussy like a good little slut."

"Theo...oh, God..." she moaned, and I could feel her convulse all around my fingers, and I almost shouted my praises to The Good Lord above.

However, I didn't let up on her. I kept my fingers pumping in and out of her pussy until she was screaming that she was going to cum again. I didn't stop until she was shivering all over and her knees started to buckle.

I pulled back and looked down at her. Her head was limp, resting against the wall, and her eyes were closed, but I could see wetness lining her lashes. It was manipulative, but I was desperate. I needed her mindless with passion being the only emotion coursing through her body. I couldn't have her sad, mad, or upset.

I leaned back down, then whispered in her ear, "Beg me to fuck you in the ass, baby. Beg me, and I promise to make you feel the best you've ever felt with my dick deep inside you."

Except for her heavy breathing, Callie's body was so still that I thought I'd lost her. However, I was wrong when her arms wrapped around my neck, and then she turned her head, crushing her lips to mine.

It was all I could do to not drop to my knees and thank God. Even if she was just making her decision based on clouded lust, I'd take it.

We were nothing but lips, tongues, hands, and fingers as we kissed in a battle for dominance. Callie's hands were at my jeans, fighting with the button and zipper, while my hands were pushing her shorts and panties down her thighs.

The second that the scent of her arousal hit me, I was walking her towards the center of the living room, tearing myself away from her long enough to position her body over the armrest of the couch.

Her drenched pussy and taut, tight, little starfish were on perfect display for me. I wasted no time taking my hard cock and slamming it into her soaked cunt. One of her hands went to the back of the couch and the other dug into the cushions as Callie's back bowed from the invasion.

It was fucking perfect.

I slammed so hard into her that I was balls-deep with one thrust. Callie was mewling and moaning into the cushions, but even as sexy as those sounds were, they weren't enough. "I said fucking beg me, Callie," I growled. Granted, I should probably take what I could get at this point, but I wanted to remind her of all the things that she wouldn't-*couldn't*-find with anyone else. Every thrust was harder than the last, and I wasn't going to let up until she said the words. "Say it," I demanded.

"Oh, God…" she moaned right before giving in. "Please, Theo…please, fuck my ass…"

Luckily, she was so wet from her previous two orgasms that all I needed to do was drop a bit of spit on that puckered hole of hers. My dick was slick as fuck, covered in all her juices, that it was already primed and ready to go. As soon as the dollop of saliva met its target, I pulled out of her cunt, then holding both her ass cheeks open wide, I pushed my cock into her ass.

My dick was so fucking hard that I didn't need to use either of my hands to help guide it into that tight hole. As soon as the head of my cock breached the ring, Callie cried out, *"Theo…"*

"Shh, baby," I said soothingly. "Relax and let my cock fill that tight ass of yours."

It took a few seconds, but Callie willed her body to stop fighting off the invasion, and soon enough, nine inches of cock was lodged deep inside her ass.

It felt like every-fucking-thing good in the world.

Though not as euphoric as fucking her pussy, knowing that I was the only man that had ever fucked Callie up the ass had me wanting to include the act constantly just to remind her of how special we were together.

"Oh, God…yes…" she wailed. "God, yes…Theo…"

I started fucking her hard, deep, and desperately. "This is why I'll never let you go," I grunted. "And this is why you'll never leave me, Callie."

"Theo, please…"

I grabbed a fistful of her hair, yanking her head back, while my other hand was busy leaving bruises on her hip. "Nothing and no one will ever feel as good as you do wrapped around my cock, baby," I told her, slamming into her, feeling her ass already clenching and gripping me. "You're allowed to rant, rail, scream, yell, hit, scratch, and fight all you want, Callie. However, the one thing that you're *not* allowed to do is leave me or make me leave."

"Theo, I'm cumming," she warned. "I'm cumming…"

The second that her body seized up and I felt that first clamp of her ass, I shot every last drop of my load deep into her hot channel. I kept slamming into her with each squirt of my release, and I didn't stop until Callie was completely limp underneath me.

After a minute or two of silence, I placed my hands on her hips, then slowly pulled my cock out of her ass. As I took a small step back, I had a clear view of her juices leaking out of her pussy and my release seeping out of her ass to mingle with her cream.

The sight was the most beautiful mess that I'd ever seen.

The fuck this was over.

We were *never* going to be over.

CHAPTER 27

The less I knew, the fucking better.

Callie ~

"Carmen's spreading a rumor that the cops had to interview you again, Ryan," Jeremiah shared as he, Brent, Lucia, Ryan, and I sat around one of the private conference rooms on our floor. We had all gathered to touch base, but as soon as the meeting was over, Beverly, Carmen, and Cody had left. I could admit that I'd been kind of surprised when Ryan had stayed behind. Now that Margot was gone, maybe he thought to soften us up to help him secure her vacancy.

Her body wasn't even cold in the ground yet, but I wasn't going to knock Ryan for doing what was best for him over a woman who had stolen the souls of the good.

Ryan leaned back in his chair and smirked. "Carmen's just trying to shift the spotlight," he replied.

My brows rose. "Why would she need to do that?"

This time, Ryan grinned. "Because, while we all couldn't stand the soulless viper, we were all still somewhat professional about it. Anytime Carmen got the chance, she talked so much shit about Margot that it was damn near professional suicide," he revealed. "During the course of the interviews, I'm sure it was pointed out, therefore, making it look like she hated Margot most out of all of us."

"Christ, she really was a horrible monster," Lucia muttered.

Ryan nodded. "That she was, Pretty Lucy," he agreed. "That she was."

Lucia shot Ryan a lethal look. "I told you to quit calling me that." He just winked at her, causing her to roll her eyes at him.

"So, you're saying the police didn't question you again, Ryan?" I asked. The man had always been a different kind of snake since the day that I'd met him, so I just didn't trust him. I wasn't saying that someone couldn't change, I just didn't believe that someone could change character so quickly.

"No, Callie, they didn't," he answered, looking directly at me. It was said that it was easy to tell when someone was playing you if you just looked them in the eye. However, if that person was a freakin' sociopath, I didn't think the saying applied.

Jeremiah's ass was perched on the table next to my chair. I wasn't sure if it was in an automatic protective gesture, but ever since Margot's murder, Jeremiah's been my shadow at work. "I just don't know what the mystery is. She got murdered in her office. It could only be a few people."

"I just wish they'd catch the person already," Lucia said. "It's kind of creepy coming to work and not knowing if the person sitting next to you is a murderer."

We all turned to look at Ryan.

He let out a strangled laugh. "Seriously, people?"

I shrugged a shoulder. "You've never done anything to me, Ryan, but it's no secret that you can be sly, slick, and wicked a lot of the time."

"Fair point, Ms. Callows," he conceded, nodding his head and not the least bit offended. "But if I were going to off that crazy bitch, it would have been when she recommended Alfred Grale for that corporate promotion after I was the one who worked on the Cinister Kemp project for over a year." I winced at that reminder.

No matter my personal opinion of Ryan, he was still a smart cookie. Very sharp, and he had busted his ass for over a year on a national medical campaign. When Cinister Kemp had fallen over themselves with glee at all of Ryan's hard work, Margot had given all the credit to Alfred Grale right in front of Ryan.

At the time, Ryan had only two choices; lose his shit and tell Margot to go fuck herself, or keep his mouth shut, remain professional, thus keeping his hopes for advancement alive.

He had opted for Door #2.

Lucia had let out a low whistle. "I'd forgotten about that."

Ryan glanced over at her. "I hadn't," he stated simply.

Brent finally chimed in. "That's actually a brilliant plan, Ryan." I looked over at him as he addressed Ryan. "Lay low for a couple of years, and then off her when no one will suspect," he suggested reasonably. "I gotta give you points for being so patient."

Ryan snorted. "Keep your points, Brent. Since I'm not the one who killed her, you should save them for the person who did."

Jay sighed. "Hell, we can't even get the details to even try to figure out who it could have been," he added. "Other than the fact that she was stabbed, the police are keeping a tight lid on all the other details."

Everyone in the room looked over at me.

"Oh, hell to the no," I said, shaking my head. "I am *not* asking Theo *anything* about Margot's case. The less I know, the fucking better."

"Oh, c'mon, Callie," Brent urged.

"Yeah, that way I can cover my tracks," Ryan joked.

Even though Jeremiah was the only person to know the details of all the shit that was going on between me and Theo, the morning of Margot's murder, everyone had recognized him from Benji's and knew that we were dating.

Or that we *had been* dating.

I still wasn't sure what we were doing exactly.

Yesterday, Theo had spent the entire night inside me, trying to make things better, using his body to do what his words couldn't, but it wasn't like I had tried to stop him. I'd wanted to get lost in him every bit as much as he'd had wanted to get lost in me. The only words that I'd spoken was when I'd been communicating what I had wanted him to do to my body. The only time that he had spoken was when he'd been communicating how I was his. The more possessive that he'd gotten, the deeper I had fallen into his trap. Had I been a stronger type of woman, I would have never let him into my condo. However, I obviously wasn't because I had.

Hell, it hadn't even taken that much convincing. The second that Theo had me up against the wall with his hand wrapped around my throat, it had been over for me. His touch was the worst kind of addiction, and once my pride had been reminded of how good he felt all around me, it had taken a huge step back, letting lust take over.

Afterwards, we had fallen asleep somewhere around two in the morning, and when he'd left me this morning, he'd done so insisting that we were going to talk about our relationship this evening and clear everything up. I'd been too tired, too exhausted, and too weak to argue.

"C'mon, you guys," I groaned. "He's not even working the case. I doubt there's anything he could tell me, even if he could-*which he wouldn't.*"

"I'm not glad she's dead, but I'm glad she's gone," Lucia blurted out, and that was probably the most accurate way to explain what we were all feeling.

"Amen, sister," Brent immediately agreed.

"Yeah, but what about the fact that we might really be working next to a murderer?" Jeremiah asked, repeating Lucia's earlier statement.

"Just because someone's killed, doesn't make them a murderer," I pointed out. "Maybe whoever killed her did it because they really just believed she needed killing and isn't just murdering for sport."

Ryan shrugged a shoulder. "Then by that logic, this person might feel justified in killing anyone who upsets them."

"Margot didn't just upset people, Ryan. She humiliated and terrorized them," Lucia countered.

"I bet you that's why corporate is waiting on announcing Margot's successor," Brent wagered. "They don't want to accidently promote a murderer."

"Make sense," I agreed. I mean, how embarrassing would it be for Melko if word got around that they had promoted a killer? Not just *any* killer, either, but the person who killed Margot to begin with?

"Well, speculating on any of this is not productive in the least," Ryan announced. "None of us knows any more than what the others know, and the hard fact is that it could have been anyone in this building and outside of it, too." He stood up, signaling that he was done with our little pow-wow, and the rest of us followed suit. As curious as we all were, we couldn't spend the day gossiping about Margot's untimely demise.

As we started filing out of the room, I felt Ryan's grip on my arm, stalling me. I turned around, then looked up at him. "You have a minute?"

I nodded and remained behind, but not before giving Jeremiah a head nod, letting him know that everything was fine. "What's up, Ryan?"

"I've always thought you were a class act, Callie. You're honest and don't play any games," he said.

"Thank you, Ryan."

His light blue eyes bore into mine. "That's why I'm..." He trailed off, looking nervous as hell. This was the first time that I'd ever seen Ryan Jones nervous. "I...I think Carmen killed Margot."

My brows rose, my eyes rounded, and I stood there staring at him completely slack-jawed.

Holy shit. Did he really believe that?

"Wh...why do you think that?"

"Because she was really, really vocal about how much she hated Margot, Callie," he explained. "I mean like very, very, *very* vocal." He lifted his left shoulder, then added, "Yeah, we all hated her, but not to the point where we couldn't continue to be professional. Carmen threw professional out the window a long time ago with all the shit she'd spew about Margot."

"I don't know, Ryan..."

"Look, I'm just telling you what I think," he replied. "Just think about it."

I did.

It was all I did for the rest of the day.

CHAPTER 28
What's the difference?

Theo ~

The Magdallini investigation was taking up a lot more time than our other cases, primarily now that our snitch was dead. The case had gone from a homicide to a multiple-connected homicide, and that's why I was knocking on Callie's door closer to nine than the agreed dinner date we'd had for six.

I had texted her earlier, and she had texted back that it was okay, but I was still wrestling with her response. While I wanted a woman that could accept the hardships of being married to a cop, it didn't sit well with me that she showed no preference if I was around or not.

Maybe it was because we still had a lot to work out.

I really wasn't sure.

I knocked, and to my gratefulness, the door swung open a few seconds later. I looked down, and Callie was standing in front of me, wearing a pair of green pajama pants, another goddamn tank top with no bra, and bare feet.

I leaned down, then kissed her temple. "You need to quit answering the door dressed like that," I muttered.

She laughed as she stepped aside, so that I could enter. "I knew it was you."

I looked back over my shoulder at her. "That's worse," I retorted. "How the hell are we supposed to talk when all I'm going to be able to do is stare at your tits?"

Callie smiled, and it was a smile designed to ruin men. "I don't mind you staring at my tits, Theo."

I let out a pained groan as my dick twitched. My cock wanted to fuck her until she forgot her own name, but we'd already done that last night. I had let us drown in lust last night, ignoring the real world, but, tonight, we needed to talk. We needed to get our shit straightened out.

Ignoring her flirting, I took a seat on her couch, then patted the space next to me in a gesture for her to sit down, too. Callie rolled her eyes as she let out a disappointed huff, but she still sat down. I laughed. Life was not going to be boring with her, that's for sure.

God, she made me crazy.

"Fine," she pouted as she flapped her hand around as if to say, 'get on with it'. I had to press my lips together before I busted out laughing at her. She was trying her best to put up a tough front, but I knew that she was still feeling hurt over our fight, no matter how many orgasms I'd given her last night.

I angled my body, so that I could face her, and she did the courtesy of doing the same. "Baby, you deserve an apology, but it's not for what you think it is," I started.

Callie crossed her legs on the couch, and she started wringing her hands together in her lap, but her eyes never strayed from mine. "It's not?"

I shook my head. "The apology you deserve and the apology you're getting is for my…failure to talk to you." She cocked her head, and the arch of her brow told me that she thought that I was full of shit. "When I was asked to talk to you about giving an interview, I should have spoken to you about it right away, and that's what I'm sorry for," I clarified. "Had I told you that I was getting pestered into convincing you and Jeremiah to give interviews, you never would have jumped to the wrong conclusion about what Darren had been talking about. That's my fault."

She was chewing the hell out of the inside of her cheek, but she finally asked, "You honestly expect me to believe that sleeping with me had nothing to do with your investigation?"

I tried not to let her question get under my skin, but it was hard. I wasn't an asshole. However, to be fair, she'd only known me a few weeks before our fight. She didn't really *know me,* know me. She just knew what she felt around me.

"I understand why you jumped to that conclusion, Callie, but you're forgetting one thing."

"Oh," she exclaimed with a full dose of snark. "And what is it that I'm forgetting *exactly?*"

I planted my hands on each of her angled knees and invaded her space as I looked her in the face. "When we fucked that first night," I said, making sure my voice was firm and absolute. "The night you let me have free reign of your delectable body, there wasn't a case yet. There hadn't been a murder, and the only thing that had been between us was skin." Her eyes darted away for a quick second, but they bravely made their way back to mine. "And it was *you* that snuck off during the morning afterwards, *not* me. I've been all in from the beginning."

Her head dropped as she let out a deep and exhausted sigh. However, I didn't push. I wanted to give her time to absorb my words and believe their implications as the truth. What we had shared that night-and every night together since then-had nothing to do with her boss' murder. Our relationship had nothing to do with anything or anyone but us. Nevertheless, I wasn't sure what I was going to do if she chose to remain stubborn about it.

Callie finally raised her head and looked at me. "Maybe you're right, Theo, but-"

"There's no *maybe* about it, Callie," I said, interrupting her. "I was not sleeping with you to try to get information about what you may or may not know about the case. *Period.*"

This time, her gaze didn't waver. "You should have told me they were pressuring you at work about me, Theo," she said. "You have no idea how I felt when I overheard you guys talking. I was crushed."

My hands reached up to cradle her face. "I know, Callie," I replied. "I know I fucked up with that. But you cannot believe I was only sleeping with you for a case, baby," I implored her. "A case that I actually gave away just to be with you."

"I know," she whispered as if I'd just pointed out that she was holding the murder weapon that killed Professor Plum in the library.

"Callie, listen to me, baby. This attraction…that crazy connection that we shared outside the restrooms at Benji's was real-*is* real. It's so fucking real, Callie. Don't let this one stupid oversight on my part ruin it." I wasn't above begging the woman.

She let out a deep sigh, causing her to shutter. "I suppose you have a point," she muttered.

I threw my head back as I laughed.

Christ, this girl.

"You suppose?"

She shrugged a dainty shoulder. "Ever since you mentioned it, that Friday night has been looping around in my mind. And thinking back on it now, you're right. The chemistry was off the charts before we even learned about each other's jobs." She sighed again. "It just sucked overhearing your conversation and thinking that it'd all been a lie."

I let go of her face, then grabbed her hands. "Callie, nothing between us is a lie. *Nothing.*"

Her green gaze searched my brown one. "You can't do that again, Theo," she pressed. "I need complete honesty from you."

I nodded. "I understand. Still, there are some things that I won't be able to tell you be-"

"Theo, I'm not asking you to give me details about your cases, or even really tell me about work," she said, interrupting me. "I get it. I really do. You deal with delicate bombs all day that require your utmost professionalism. What I'm asking from you is honesty, not confidences."

"What's the difference?"

"I know your work is dangerous and erratic, and I'm not going to try to change that about your career-about *you*. But, for example, if you get assigned a job that's a little more out of the scope of your everyday danger, and you have to go in and bust high level…uh…criminals, drug dealers…something…well, I expect you to come home and tell me that you landed a dangerous case. However, I don't expect the names, dates, and details of what that case entails. I just need to know if you're going to be in harm's way…or more serious than usual."

The pang in my chest rendered me speechless for a few seconds. Callie sounded like she was more than ready to embrace the pitfalls of being involved with a cop, but I had to be sure. "So, you're saying that as long as I'm honest with you about everything, minus case details, you're in? Because I gotta tell you, Callie, I'm going to be out of your bed more times than I'm going to be in it. I'm going to eat fast food more times than I'll be sitting at the dinner table with you. I'm going to miss parties, company events, and a shitload of other things people with real lives do."

She arched a brow. "Are you saying that I have the option to back out right now?" she teased.

"No," I answered, not teasing at all. "You don't get any options anymore."

Callie leaned forward, then planted the softest kiss on my lips. The kiss felt like it could be a kiss for the future or a goodbye kiss; it was just so sweet and tender. When she was done, she pulled back, leaving only an inch or so between our faces. I wanted her in my face like this every day. "I'm sorry for not giving you a chance to explain earlier. As hurtful as it was, I shouldn't have been a coward, and I should have faced the problem head-on. If you can promise to be completely honest from now on, I can promise to try not to flip out until I know the whole story."

I reached for her, forcing her to untangle her legs, then hauled her up to straddle my lap. My hands found the outside of her thighs, and I rubbed them back and forth. She looped her arms around my neck, smiling down at me. "It's hard to date someone that's never around, Callie." I wasn't trying to talk her out of being with me-*God, I wasn't*-but she wanted honesty and that was about as honest as it got.

"I'm sure it is," she agreed. "But I want to try."

"You were never getting a choice," I reminded her.

She snorted. "It's a good thing you have such a big dick, Theo."

Yes, it was.

It was a good thing, indeed.

CHAPTER 29
Nope.

Callie~

This wasn't the first time that I'd had to work late, and I was sure it wouldn't be my last. However, it *was* the first time that I'd had to stay late after someone had been murdered, and it was giving me the freakin' willies. Granted, I wasn't alone in the building, so that was something. Marlon was still downstairs at the security booth.

The part that had me all heeby-jeebied out was that I had to set up the top floor conference room for a new employee H.R. relations overhaul. In light of all the interviews, my diary log, and the popular opinion that Margot had been an unapologetic asshole, the company had decided that each location needed a refresher on workplace harassment and Melko policies regarding the topic.

The building had started to thin out a few days ago and a lot of corporate people had gone back to Baltimore. The company was pushing us to go back to business as usual, and that included not needing extra security in the building. Now, had it been up to me, I would have waited until the killer had been caught. However, it hadn't been up to me, and I knew that having this place swarmed with extra security and corporate employees had been costing a pretty penny. Plus, I didn't want to look like a pussy by asking someone to stay over with me. I knew Jeremiah, Brent, or even Lucia would have stayed with me, but I felt like I needed to show a solid front.

I looked down at the presentation tools and pamphlets, and I knew that I'd have to make a second trip, and that sucked because I sure as hell wanted to get out of here. So, I gathered my materials and cradled as many items to my chest as possible, then headed for the elevator. Corporate had implemented the keycard policy to Margot's precious top floor, and so now everyone needed an employee badge to access her floor. A little too late, but what could you do?

The elevator doors slid open, and as I stepped out onto Margot's floor, I noticed a faint glow coming from inside of her office. Well, I supposed I should quit referring to it as Margot's, but old habits and all.

My shoes made no noise across the plush carpet, and I was ready to call out, so that I didn't startle anyone, but when I rounded the corner, I saw Cory standing in Margot's office.

Only he wasn't standing.

Nope.

He appeared to be searching around the office for something, and Cody should *not* be in Margot's office looking for anything.

As a matter of fact, I was pretty certain that no one's been in that office but our interim. While the crime scene had been cleaned up, Corporate H.R. had thought it would be best if the room remained free of traffic in case investigators had to come back and look around again.

I turned left towards the conference room, then placed everything on the table. Cody couldn't see me from here and the sounds from the room didn't carry across the floor. I was pretty certain Cody thought that he was alone up here, and for the life of me, I couldn't imagine what business he had in that office.

I decided to find out.

My feet were silent as I approached Margot's office, and Cody was so engaged in whatever he was looking for that he hadn't looked up at all as I took up the doorway. "Cody?"

His head snapped up, and for a split second, I didn't recognize his face. His blonde hair that was usually combed to hipster perfection was standing on end. It looked as if he'd been running his hands through it, attempting to yank it out. His normally bright blue eyes looked wild and panicked. His face was pale even, and the kid's complexion was usually as white as snow, so that was saying something.

I was immediately alarmed. "Cody, what's wrong?"

"Ca…Callie…" he stammered. "What are…are…you doing here?"

I jerked my head towards the direction of the conference room. "I had to set up for the H.R. revamp tomorrow," I answered casually, even though I was feeling anything *but.*

Now, I could remember back when I was maybe eight or nine-years-old, my father had been teaching me how to fish. I remembered not being interested in going, but he had argued that life wasn't an entitlement, and that I had to learn how to fend for myself, should I ever find myself in a situation where food, clothing, shelter, medicine, etc. wasn't readily available to me. At that young of an age, the concept had terrified me, and once that horrifying possibility had taken residence up in my head, I had been eager to learn how to fish.

It was during this apocalyptic quality bonding time that my father had explained that fishing was a sport of patience and had explained that we could spend all day at the creek and still not catch anything. When I had asked him why, he had gone on to explain about animal instincts. He'd told me that your gut instinct triggered for a reason and that I should never ignore it; it could be the difference between living and dying.

Well, my gut instinct was screaming at me right now.

Ssscccrrrreeeeeeeeammmmmmminnnnng.

I prayed that he couldn't hear the rush of my blood or the pounding of my heart. I prayed that I sounded as nonchalant and casual as possible. That being said, I decided to try to bond with Cody. I gave a light laugh, trying to put him at ease. "In light of the interviews depicting Margot as evil incarnate, Corporate H.R. decided we needed to reassess the company's H.R. practices to make sure another Margot doesn't slip through the cracks."

Cody's face was still pale, and his eyes still wild, but now his eyes were kind of laced with sadness. "She was so horrible, Callie," he said softly. "I mean, she was really a horrible, horrible, horrible person."

I stayed in the doorway, not daring to inch farther into the room, as I continued to feel him out. "Yeah," I agreed. "She was awful. Thankfully, she's gone now, Cody. We don't have to be subjected to her cruelty any longer."

His face turned from pale and confused to red and livid before I could even register it happening. "It's *not* over, Callie," he spat. "Don't you get that? Just because the bitch is dead, it doesn't mean she's still not ruining people's lives."

You know that stupid, big-breasted, bikini-wearing idiot in horror flicks that never had the sense to save herself? Well, that was me right now because, while every nerve in my body was screaming at me to turn around and run the hell away from Cody's obvious breakdown, my brain was failing me, telling me to stay and find out what he was talking about.

I remained standing inside the doorway, but I didn't make any attempt to move forward or step backwards. Instead, I just asked, "Cody, what are you talking about? Margot is gone."

He took a deep breath, straightened his spine, then cocked his head at me. This was not the Cody that I knew; the Cody that we all knew. This was a different Cody. One who appeared strong, confident, and controlled. I couldn't see any signs of the weak, kiss-ass, pleaser that I was used to.

This was bad.

Cody planted his hands flat against the desk, then leaned in towards me. "You think Margot's gone?" He didn't let me reply. "Because I've got news for you, Callie. *She's not.*"

I wrapped my arms around my waist, trying to find something to do with my hands. "Wh…what do you mean, Cody? Of course, she's gone."

I wouldn't have believed it if I hadn't seen it for myself, but one second, Cody was leaning across the desk, glaring at me, then the next, he was throwing his arms across the desk, wiping everything onto the floor. "Until I can find that goddamn video, she's not gone!" he roared. "She's still here! She's still ruining my life, Callie!" Spit was flying everywhere as Cody was becoming unhinged. "You can't kill evil! I know that now!"

I took one step back but kept my eyes on Cody. "What'd she do to you, Cody?" I was genuinely curious, but I also wanted to buy myself some time. Something told me that if I turned around and started running, he would chase, and there was no telling what he'd do then.

I didn't know this person.

His hands were balled into fists at his sides, and I could tell he was struggling to come to terms with reality. "She has a video of me…"

Oh, God.

"She's got a video of me, and I need to get it back, Callie." His face went from rage to desperation, and it was sort of amazing how he was a kaleidoscope of emotions right now. "I need to find it," he repeated.

Turn around you fucking idiot! Turn around and fucking run!

"What's supposedly on the video, Cody?"

Who gives a fuck what's on that tape? RUN!

His face was contorted with anger and…hurt. "She…Margot…"

For the love of all that's holy, run, you stupid fool!

Cody let out a ragged breath. "One night, I was less than discrete and forgot about the stupid security camera Margot ordered for the supply rooms to prevent theft," he revealed brokenly.

There was only one reason-well, two reasons-actually three reasons-why that would be a problem. First, you didn't want to lose your job. Second, you and your indiscretion were married-to *other* people. Third, your indiscretion would reveal your…uh, preferences.

"Cody…"

He slammed his palms down on the desk, and he looked so devastated. "I need that fucking video, Callie. Where is it?"

I could feel my eyes widen. "Cody, I have no idea where th-"

"Bullshit!" he raged unreasonably.

It was then that I finally ran my ass out of there.

CHAPTER 30
I love you.

Theo ~

It was a scene that I'd seen a million times, but it still made my skin tingle underneath the surface, and Darren claimed it was what made me a good cop. He said it was a good thing that I hadn't been desensitized to the evils of the world. He warned me that if the day ever came that I wasn't bothered by a murder scene, then I should quit the force because there was a fine line between catching monsters and becoming one of them.

"I guess we finally know who killed the Magdallini Girl and Chaz," Darren stated solemnly.

The apartment was blocked off by your bold, traditional, yellow crime scene tape, and the place was swarming with CSI, collecting evidence, conducting interviews, and taking photos. Darren and I had done our usual song and dance of surveying the place, but this massacre essentially closed two of our cases.

It helped that the person responsible for the multiple deaths of Lena Magdallini and Chaz Earlmyer, and these two sprawled out on the couch, each with a bullet hole in their heads, was handcuffed in one of the police cruisers downstairs.

Darren and I had been called to the scene because we were the point detectives for both Lena and Chaz's murders and, apparently, the lunatic handcuffed in the cruiser had confessed and was still confessing to anyone who would listen if the screeching from the backseat of the squad car was any indication.

Officer Grant Hendricks had been the first responding officer on the scene, and after approaching us with the customary shaking of hands, gave us the rundown. "We got a call from a neighbor complaining of screaming and excessive noise, like a fight or something was going on inside the apartment. Brinkley and I were en route when we got another call from dispatch, this one stating that the same neighbor who had called with the initial complaint had called back, claiming she heard shots being fired."

"Looks like she was right," Darren muttered.

"So, then, what?" I asked, cutting to the chase.

"We came in and the two victims were already deceased on the couch while the perpetrator had been sitting over in that armchair-" Grant jerked his chin towards an ugly, lime-green armchair that had seen better days. "-just as sweet as you please."

"The gun?" I knew that there was no way that she'd still been holding it. They would have shot her dead if she'd had been.

"It was laying on the coffee table with the safety on," Grant smirked. "All responsible like."

"So, the names of this starring cast?" I looked the victims over, and I didn't recognize either of them.

Grant pulled out his standard-issue spiral notebook and recited what he knew. "The lunatic handcuffed downstairs is Heidi Verona. The two vics are Samuel Holgrim and Judith Earlmyer."

My head swung back towards Grant. *"Earlmyer?"*

"Yep," he confirmed. "Best we know right now, she was Chaz Earlmyer's wife."

"Sonofabitch," Darren breathed out. "How did we not know that he had a fucking wife?"

"Probably because the best we can figure from the ramblings of Madam Lunatic, she had left Chaz years ago, but never filed for divorce. However, she was using her maiden name, though not legally."

I ran my hands through my hair as I let out a deep breath. "Okay, okay," I uttered, trying to collect my thoughts. "You said that Ms. Verona's been a fountain of information since you guys got here. Did she mention why she killed Lena Magdallini, Chaz, then these two?"

Grant rolled his lips inward, pressing them into a tight grimace. His next words were sure to send me and Darren off for some much-needed drinks. "According to Ms. Murder U.S.A-" I briefly closed my eyes. Hendricks was so unprofessional sometimes, but I got it. Some of us had to keep things light or go crazy. "-it's a tale as old as time, guys."

"Money?" Darren prompted.

"Jealousy?" I added.

"Ding, ding, ding," he parodied. "And the winner is Detective Marsden."

Jesus Christ. People were so stupid.

"Once we secured the scene, we sat her down, then she quickly explained how she had accidentally shot Lena Magdallini, thinking she was Judith Earlmyer. Apparently, Ms. Verona likes to slum it, and she'd been carrying on an affair with Chaz Earlmyer for some time. She heard Chaz was visiting with Judith, and she lost her shit."

"Are you fucking serious?" Darren barked. "Lena Magdallini is over twenty years younger than Chaz. There's no way that she was getting it on with that guy." He shook his head. "Nah, I don't believe it. By all accounts, Lena Magdallini was a good girl. How could Ms. Verona even assume that?"

"I have to agree with Darren on this, Hendricks," I added.

"Well, that's where it gets all unfortunate and it makes you wonder about God's plan for some people," he answered. "According to Ms. Verona, which is according to what she claims Chaz told her, Lena and Samuel Holgrim went to community college together, and Lena was out one night with Samuel, where they ran into Judith. Lena went outside to smoke, and Chaz joined her. Ms. Verona had a habit of stalking Chaz, and she came up on them outside the club together, and after a few heated words, she pulled out her piece and shot the poor girl."

"Motherfucker," Darren hissed. "It was never gang-related. Chaz had sent us on a unicorn hunt."

Grant nodded in agreement, and then continued with his accounts. "Once Ms. Verona found out Lena wasn't Judith, she lost her shit and shot Chaz. Then, as soon as she realized that she hadn't made any efforts to cover her tracks, she went the Thelma and Louise route and stalked Judith Earlmyer until she found her here with Samuel Holgrim, then shot them both."

"Lena and Samuel were really just in the wrong place at the wrong time," I stated unnecessarily.

"Yep," Grant concurred. "Had absolutely nothing to do with drugs or gangs or any of that shit. Just some crazy ass broad in love."

I scanned the apartment again. "And this is Samuel's place?"

"Yeah."

"How did Samuel know Judith? There's a huge age gap for them to be friends, no?" Darren posed.

"That's what I thought, but then after we started searching the residence and questioning the neighbors, it looks like Samuel and Judith were the ones sleeping together, not Lena and Chaz." Grant chuckled. "I guess age is just a number, boys."

I snorted. "You know what else is just a number? Your inmate identification."

Hendricks laughed. "Hey, now, young Samuel was legal, and you know what they say about older women? They're an endless fountain of useful knowledge and experience."

"An older man with a younger woman is creepy, but an older woman with a younger man is educational?" Darren quipped, shaking his head. "It's just not right."

"Even if they're the same age, women will always be older than men," I countered. "They mature way faster, and The Good Lord knows that they're a hell of a lot smarter than us."

"Amen, brother," Grant muttered. "Amen."

"That's because you two are idiots," Darren disagreed.

"My man, the idiot is the man who thinks-*for even a second*-that women are the weaker sex," Grant stated wisely, and neither of us argued. "So, back to murder, mayhem, and flat-out psychopathic tendencies. We'll drive her back to the station where you guys can officially question her and close your cases."

"Thanks, man. See you back at the house." I shook his hand, then headed for the door. Darren was right behind me after shaking Grant's hand in a farewell.

As we made our way down the stairs and out of the building, we paused for a second, so that Darren could light a cigarette. He didn't smoke often, usually only once we closed a case. He equated it to how some people smoked after sex; he smoked after we closed a case.

A strange one, that man.

My phone started ringing, and I immediately recognized the ring tone. It was Callie, and I couldn't stop the stupid grin that spread across my face. I ignored Darren as he called me pussy-whipped and answered, "Hey, baby."

"Theo," she whispered, and the hairs on the back of my neck stood up.

"Callie, what's wrong?"

"Theo, I think I know who killed Margot," she whispered, shocking the holy fucking shit out of me.

"What?" I could feel Darren tense beside me.

"I was upstairs-"

"Callie, where are you now?" I needed to know if she was in danger. I could find out the rest later.

"I'm locked in my office, and I'm hiding the best way I know how."

My body felt like it was going to explode. A fear like I'd never felt before seemed like it was too explosive to hold in. "Callie, listen to me, okay?" I didn't wait for her confirmation. "Push your desk, a bookcase, whatever you can, up against the door. I don't give a fuck if it's locked. Make that motherfucker impenetrable. I'm on my way, Callie."

"Theo?"

"Yeah, baby?"

"I love you."

CHAPTER 31
Well. Fuck. Me. Running.

Callie ~

I could admit that I might have personified that dumb chick in the horror flick earlier, but once my feet got going and common sense had taken over, I had run for my office, then locked the door behind me. The second that the lock had engaged, I had dialed 911, then tried not to panic at the thumps and bangs being battered against the door, but I was scared. Cody had been screaming my name, and thankfully, he'd been loud enough for the 911 operator to have heard him through the phone. I hadn't had to do a whole lot of explaining, and the second that I'd hung up with her, I had dialed Theo.

As soon as we'd disconnected, I shoved at my desk to see if I could move it across the room, and while it was heavy as hell, I had adrenaline to thank for helping me move the damn thing. I almost had it against the door when I heard a muffled cry, and it sounded like my name.

I was leaning forward, ready to press my ear up against the door to try to hear...well, anything...when a sudden thump against the door had me jumping back. "Callie! Are you in there?"

Oh, my God.

That sounded like Carmen's voice, but...where was Cody?

"Callie, please!" she cried, her voice coming through the door again.

I raced around the desk, then turned the lock as quickly as I could. It was clearly evident that Cody had lost his goddamn mind, and there was no telling what he'd do to Carmen if my assumptions about him killing Margot were correct.

I swung the door open, and Carmen stood there, looking frantic and haggard. "Carmen!"

Her eyes widened and the relief on her face was clear. "Callie, oh God...I think-"

I didn't let her finish her sentence. I reached out, then grabbing her by her arm, I yanked her inside my office. Not even bothering to check to see where

129

she landed, I slammed the door shut, then locked it again.

The desk was still a bit of a distance from the door, so I looked over at Carmen and said, "Here, help me move this up against the door. I've already called the cops, but…Jesus, Carmen, Cody has lost his mind, and I think he killed Margot."

She started shaking her head in disbelief. "Why would he kill Margot? What possible motive could he have, Callie? This is Cody Buckner we're talking about."

Christ.

If I was that stupid fool that didn't know when to run from a killer, Carmen was the stupid fool that was asking for an explanation when it could totally wait until we were safe. Too bad I needed her convinced, so that we could get out of this alive. Well…to be fair, I wasn't sure if Cody had a weapon or anything. However, I knew enough to know that he scared me, and if it was possible that he did kill Margot, then there was nothing stopping him from killing me for catching him in her office. If nothing else, if Cody wasn't armed, I was sure that Carmen and I could probably kick his ass, but I needed her on my side before I organized an offensive attack on the man.

"Carmen, help me with this desk. *Please,*" I implored.

She stood in the middle of the room, twisting her hands together and fidgeting nervously. "Callie, please tell me what's going on? I thought I heard someone screaming or yelling or something. Was it Cody?"

God, I didn't have fucking time for this.

"I was setting up some meeting materials for the Corporate H.R. overhaul tomorrow, and I caught Cody snooping around in Margot's office," I explained hurriedly. "He started yelling at me about a video that he was looking for and it just got…crazy after that. *He* got crazy."

"Did he say what was on the video? Do you know if he found it?" she asked.

"Oh, for fuck's sakes, Carmen," I snapped. "Who gives a fuck about the video? He could possibly be the person who murdered Margot, and if his ranting and raving and coming after me are any indication, I'd say that he murdered Margot for whatever is on that video. Nevertheless, what we need to do now is protect ourselves until the police get here."

"And you've already called the police?"

I was getting so exasperated with her horror flick dumb girl act that I stopped worrying about the desk, turning to finally get a good look at her.

Well. Fuck. Me. Running.

The closer that I regarded her, the more I realized that Carmen didn't look like a woman scared and running from a lunatic. She didn't look like someone in shock at finding out that one of her co-workers could possibly be a murderer.

Nope.

She looked like someone trying to put all the pieces together before calculating their next move.

Sonofabitch.

It appeared as if I was on the wrong side of the goddamn door.

I had two choices here: I could either run for the door with the possibility of Cody being on the other side, or I could stay in here, try to keep her talking, and then kick her fucking ass if she comes at me. Hell, I should probably just kick her ass for all the grief that she was causing me right now. However, I didn't know Carmen all that well, and for all I knew about her, she might be a master at Taekwondo or some such shit.

"Carmen..." *Fuck it.* "What's going on? What's on that video?" The transformation was incredible. I watched as Carmen went from a nervous, confused, worried damsel in distress to a strong, unafraid, cold bitch. "What the fuck, Carmen?"

She shrugged a shoulder as she smirked. "I suppose it doesn't matter," she replied coldly. "It's not like I'm going to let you live, and I sure as fuck am not going to let you escape this room. And, yes, Cody is standing right on the other side of the door."

"You guys killed Margot," I deduced, not really talking to her, just talking out loud.

Carmen snickered. "Seriously, Callie?" she huffed, rolling her eyes. "Do you really think Cody is capable of *killing* someone? The man's milk toast."

"Okay. I'm game," I said, tired of her shit. "I'm in agreement with you about Cody being a pussy, so that must mean that it was you who killed Margot." It wasn't a question or a guess.

Carmen cocked her head, and her smile was telling. "I've always known that you didn't like me much, Callie. That you lumped me in with Cody, Beverly, and Ryan as a bunch of company ass kissers." I didn't deny it. If I was going to die-or get my ass kicked-it wasn't going to be as a lying wimp. "However, be that as it may, I don't mind telling you why Margot had to go."

I snorted.

I couldn't stop myself.

"You can quit with the theatrics, Carmen. There are a million reasons why the world is better off without Margot," I retorted. "Your one reason is probably the least of them."

She lifted a brow as if I had offended her somehow, but went on to explain, nonetheless. "One night, Cody and I were working late, and we kind of got carried away in one of the storage rooms," she confessed, shocking the shit out of me. While Carmen was a nice-looking woman, she was married and forty-two-years-old to Cody's twenty-eight years of age. Their hookup would not have been anything that I would have ever predicted.

"So, Margot was blackmailing you with the security footage?" I asked, even though it really wasn't a question, but more of a conclusion to her story.

"Not exactly," she replied. "When she called us up to her office to confront us about the video feed, she went on to blackmail us into continuing to…uh, perform for her in random rooms of the building." I couldn't stop my gasp of incredulousness. "It wasn't until she upped the ante that I decided to put a stop to it."

"What'd she do?" I whispered in complete shock. I mean, I knew that Margot had been a nasty piece of work, but she'd also been a pervert on top of being a conning witch?

"Margot threatened to tell my husband if Cody didn't…" Her gaze faltered for a fraction of a second, but just one fraction. "She wanted Cody to fuck her in some sick recreation of all our times together," she confessed. "She wanted to act out each of our videos."

Holy…what?

"So, you killed her to save your marriage," I concluded.

Carmen shook her head. "No, Callie," she snapped. "I couldn't give a fuck about my husband. If I did, then I wouldn't be screwing Cody. I killed that miserable, selfish, horrible cow because there was no way that I was going to let her have Cody. He might be a pussy, but…he makes me feel special."

"Then why not just let her tell your husband?!" I yelled, confused as hell.

"I might not give a shit about him, but a divorce would have a devastating financial impact on my life!" she yelled back.

"Carmen!" The yelling and thumping on the door startled me, causing me to jump back into the corner.

It was Cody, and if Carmen let him in, I was done for. There was no way I could take them both. If she killed for him, there was a good chance that he might feel indebted to her and kill for her in return.

In this one decisive moment in time, I thought about Theo. I thought about how I'd just told him that I loved him and how much I actually meant it. Finding a good man was akin to finding a unicorn at the end of a rainbow that was hanging out with a leprechaun around a pot of gold. So, there was no way that I was going to let these two stupid fuckers ruin that for me.

As soon as Carmen made her way towards the door, flight took a backseat to fight, and I charged the bitch like the badass that I really was not.

CHAPTER 32
Holy shit!

Theo ~

Darren and I were going to arrive at the Melko building before anyone else. As soon as we'd gotten into the car, Darren had contacted dispatch to confirm if Callie had put in a call to 911. Their confirmation hadn't done anything in determining my speed and desperation to get to Melko, but it helped knowing that there was going to be some backup soon enough.

Her last words felt like spikes being driven through my chest over and over again. Callie hadn't told me that she loved me because the moment had been right. No. She'd told me that she loved me because she didn't think that she'd get a chance to tell me later, and that thought had my blood running cold and my fury running hot.

This wasn't how this was supposed to go down. Callie was supposed to have told me that she loved me while cuddled in my arms in bed. She was supposed to have told me that she loved me after I told her that I loved her. I'd had it all planned. I was going to spend the weekend fucking her until she wouldn't ever run from me again, and then we were going to profess our love for one another and be married by Monday.

I was going to fuck someone up for fucking with my weekend plans.

We were still about five minutes away when the car almost fishtailed as I came around the corner, not giving a fuck about the public's safety.

"Goddamn it, Theo," Darren growled. "You're not going to be able to help her if you kill us on the way to Melko."

"There's no way we're dying," I argued. "At least, not before I get to Callie."

I could feel my partner's stare as I focused on the road ahead of us. "But once she's safe, then you're okay with the dying part?" he deadpanned.

"If she's safe, then I am," I answered truthfully. "But don't worry, Dar. I plan on living a long, healthy, happy life. There's no way I'll let Callie live on without me."

Darren snorted out a laugh. "That's good to hear, Stud. I happen to like my life."

Five minutes and a shitload of avoided car collisions later, I was banging on the Melko building's front door. Luckily, Darren had his badge out and was holding it up against the glass as the security guard walked his way over.

However, even with Darren showing his badge, the motherfucker didn't open the doors, instead opting to speak to us through the glass. "How may I help you?" he asked, not even bothering to study Darren's badge.

"Open the fucking doors!" I bellowed loud enough for the people on the next block to hear me, not giving one fuck about professionalism.

The asshole just crossed his arms over his chest.

"We're Detectives Marsden and Franklin!" Darren yelled. "We got a call from an employee inside the building! A 911 emergency!"

I was two seconds away from shattering the entire door when the guard's eyes widened, finally grasping that we were serious and that this wasn't some kind of prank or company exercise. He reached for his keys, then hurried to open the doors. He stepped aside, barely escaping getting mowed over.

"Callie Callows," I snapped. "Where's her office?"

"Uh…uhm, she's on the fourteenth floor, but-"

I didn't wait for him to finish. I was already running for the stairwell as I heard Darren briefing the guard that more police would be showing up in a matter of minutes. I was pushing the elevator button for all that I was worth, knowing that Darren was giving the guard the proper rundown of what was happening.

The elevator dinged, and I didn't even wait for the doors to open all the way. I was already pushing the button for the fourteenth floor when Darren rushed past the elevator towards the stairwell. It was moments like these that I thanked God that my partner and I were so in tuned.

I stood in the goddamn elevator looking up at the floor numbers as they turned, but not turning nearly fast enough. If my math was right-and it could be wrong because my mind was a fucking wreck-it'd been a good twenty minutes since I'd gotten that call from Callie, and that was twenty minutes too fucking long. I also hadn't called her back because I wanted all her concentration to be centered on staying safe and not having to worry about answering my calls. I also didn't want to alert Margot's killer to Callie's whereabouts.

Now, while Callie hadn't said much, she'd said that she thought she knew who killed Margot and that she was hiding in her office. That meant that she must have stumbled upon someone or something she shouldn't have. Now, if she was hiding in her office, I could only deduce that it was a 'someone' that she had stumbled upon, and now she was in danger. I could only pray that she had listened to me and had barricaded herself inside her office. I wouldn't know what I'd do if she wasn't okay. There was a good chance that I'd lose my badge and my freedom if Callie wasn't okay.

The elevator finally hit the fourteenth floor, and I was out of there before the doors fully opened. Luckily, I was familiar with the layout of the floor from our initial crime scene visit when this had been mine and Darren's case. I knew exactly where the H.R. offices were located, I just didn't know which one was Callie's office. For whatever fucking reason-probably Margot Livingston's sociopathic ways-there were no identifiers on the doors. The offices were just labeled as H.R., Accounting, Research, etc.

Running like the promise of my life was at the finish line, I rounded the corner at top speed and saw Cody Buckner standing in front of one of the doors, pounding away on it.

I pulled out my gun, aimed, and kept running. "Freeze!" Cody startled and turned at my booming command. "You move one motherfucking inch, and I will blow a hole in you so big that it'll take weeks to gather all your pieces." Cody immediately threw his hands up in the air and froze. "Where is she? Where's Callie?"

I heard Darren's footsteps behind me, and his command thundered down the hallway. "Get down on your knees now!"

As soon as I stood in front of Cody, I asked again, "Where the fuc-" I stopped when I heard noises coming from behind the office door. "Callie!" I started banging on the wood as Darren handcuffed Cody behind me, securing him in place.

"Theo!" came faintly from behind the door and that was all I needed.

I stepped back, then kicked the fucking door in, praying that there was no barricade this time. The wood around the door frame splintered, but it took one more kick to break the door open off the lock. "Callie!" I ran in and the sight before me left me momentarily stunned.

H.R. Manager, Callie Callows-*my Callie*-was straddled over a woman that I couldn't make out and was stone-cold beating the crap out of her.

Holy shit!

I shook myself out of my stupor, then ran into the room. I grabbed Callie off the unknown woman, then set her behind me. My first instinct was to gather Callie up in my arms and just hold on, but I didn't know the woman on the floor, and I had no idea if she was armed or not. I just knew that she was one of the bad guys if Callie was kicking her ass.

Every second counted in my line of work, so instead of gathering Callie into my arms and making sure that she was okay, I went for the woman on the floor to secure her before she could shoot us all or escape. Darren stood in the doorway, holding Cody in custody as I picked the woman up, handcuffed her, then held onto her to keep her from trying to run.

As soon as I had my hand wrapped around her arm, I heard Darren say, "In here." I turned to see a uniformed patrolman entering the room. It was another one of those moments that I was glad that Darren and I were in sync; he knew that I needed to hold my girl right now.

I still had my back to Callie when Darren instructed the uniformed officer to watch Cody. When a second officer entered the room, Darren took the woman in hand, and that's when I finally turned around and pulled Callie into my arms.

"Goddamn it, baby," I whispered hoarsely.

Callie wrapped her arms around me, then muffled into my chest, "Carmen…Carmen killed Margot, not Cody. It was Carmen."

I looked over at Darren that had-*who I presumed was Carmen*-seated in the desk chair with his hand firmly resting on her shoulder. I jerked my head in her direction, saying, "She killed Ms. Livingston."

Callie unwrapped herself from my torso-I didn't like it-then turned to face Carmen and Darren. "She admitted to killing Margot. She told me it was her, not Cody."

Darren nodded at her. "Well, they'll both be going down to the station to be questioned." Then he kind of grimaced. "You'll have to go, too, Callie."

Carmen's head started whipping around, her eyes momentarily landing on each one of us. "What in the fuck is this? You assholes barge in here and see *her* assaulting *me,* but *I'm* the one in handcuffs? Why isn't she being arrested, too? I want to file charges!"

I took in Carmen's appearance, and she looked a bit muffed up, but aside from a busted lip, some reddening on her left cheek, and her hair looking all to hell, she didn't look too bad. I stared straight into this bitch's face and said, "I didn't see anything like you described." She let out a drama-worthy gasp-*as she should*-because I was teetering on the line of the law right now. "I saw Ms. Callows defending herself against a murderer. Detective Franklin?"

"That's what it looked like to me," Darren agreed like I knew that he would, like I loved the man for. Carmen started screaming, but I ignored her as Darren walked her out.

I turned back to Callie. I raked my eyes all over her body to make sure that she was okay before demanding, "Don't you *ever* do that to me again."

CHAPTER 33
The dick.

Callie ~

It didn't matter if you were guilty or innocent. For me, sitting in a police station always gave me the heeby-jeebies. Granted, it could be from watching too much Investigation Discovery, but still.

Right now, I knew that I was being viewed as a victim and my recount of what happened was going to make or break the case against Carmen. However, my mind couldn't help but wander back, trying to recall if I had any outstanding parking tickets.

It wasn't that I was anti-police, but I wasn't pro-police, either. They were a part of our societal structure that I accepted, but never paid much attention to. Luckily, I'd never had to. I'd never gotten in trouble before or ran with criminals.

Well, except for that one time when it came out that I was working with a murderer…or murderess, rather. Yeah. Except for that one time.

It also didn't help that I'd been sitting in this goddamn cage of a room for over an hour without being checked on. I mean, Jesus, that was just plain ass rude. You'd think me dating a cop would warrant me a cup of tea or a cup of water, but I guess the only true benefit to dating Theo was his readily access to a pair of handcuffs.

Once I'd told Theo that Carmen had been the one that had killed Margot, Detective Franklin had escorted her downstairs into one of the squad cars. As I'd taken in the scene of flashing lights and the sea of cops, I'd seen Cody handcuffed in the back of one of the cars already.

I hadn't wanted to ride in a cop car back to the police station, so Theo had made a solemn promise to drive me back himself in my car. Detective Franklin had driven their car behind the cars carrying Carmen and Cody, Theo and I trailing behind him.

As soon as we had entered the building, we'd been met by Detectives Ridley and Horrace, then I'd been immediately ushered into one of the interrogation rooms. Detective Ridley had asked me to take a seat, said he'd be right back, and that was over an hour ago.

The dick.

I was so hoping that it was going to be Detective Horrace that would come back for my statement. Detective Ridley came off as a bit of a douche.

Another twenty minutes had passed before the door finally opened and both detectives walked in. I watched silently as they made their way inside the room, then each taking a seat across from me. I was so goddamn irritated that I was seriously ready to just walk the fuck out. It was late as hell, and I was starving, cold, thirsty, and the adrenaline from tonight had finally worn off. Honestly, I was just plain damn exhausted, and these two jackholes had decided to keep me sitting in here for almost an hour and a half without bothering to send someone to check on me or checking on me themselves. Good thing that I'd hadn't had to go pee.

"Ms. Callo-"

The second that Detective Ridley spoke, irritation and immaturity took over. I held my hand up to silence the man. "Let me stop you there, Detective," I interrupted. "I am going home-"

"What?" This time, Detective Ridley did the interrupting.

I gave him my best mean mug. "You escorted me into this room over an hour and a half ago, Detective, and not once, during that entire time, have either of you come in here to check on me, or offer me anything to drink or eat as I waited." I watched as they both exchanged an uneasy glance. "So, due to your blatant rudeness, I'm going the hell home. I'm going to walk out of this room, grab whichever fast food is on the way to my house, eat, take a hot shower, go to sleep, wake up, get ready for work, then depending on how the company decides to deal with all this, I might put in a full day's work, I might not."

"Ms. Call-"

"Stop, Detective Horrace. You cannot undo your rudeness at this point," I complained. "Once I am done with my workday, I will put in a call to Bianca Milton and ask her if she, or Mr. Milton, can accompany me down here to speak with you gentlemen." I said the word 'gentlemen' with a sneer because I was just so damn tired, hungry, and irritated.

"Don't make us arrest you, Ms. Callows," Detective Ridley threatened.

I arched a brow.

To hell with this dude.

"For what exactly, Detective Ridley?"

"Failure to cooperate. Assault on Mrs. Carmen Randall. Take your pick." He leaned back in his chair, then crossed his arms over his chest like he'd just won the match.

Okay, never mind sending him to hell.

Fuck. This. Dude.

"Okay." I held both my wrists out. "Arrest me," I dared him. "But might I suggest that you don't forget to read me my Rights first."

I could see Detective Ridley's jaw tick, and I knew that he was pissed that I had called him on his bluff. "Do you think I'm playing, Ms. Callows?"

I leaned forward because I had no sense of self-preservation. However, they were treating me like a criminal, and I wasn't having it. Still, I finally understood why they used waiting as an interrogation tool. A person would say just about anything to get some food, sleep, or something to drink. "Do you think that *I'm* playing, Detective Ridley?"

Detective Horrace finally intervened. "Okay, okay. Let's all just calm down a bit." He turned his gaze towards me. *"Please."*

"Oh, so, *now,* you want to exercise good manners?" I replied flippantly.

"Ms. Call-"

"We thought Theo wou-"

"Why would Theo babysit me?" I turned my eyes towards Detective Ridley. "This isn't his case."

Detective Ridley closed his eyes, then threw his head back. I couldn't make out his mumbling, but I was pretty sure that he was praying to Jesus, Our Lord and Savior.

"Ms. Callows, how about this?" Detective Horrace said, ignoring his partner's praying. "What if we ask Detective Marsden to bring you something to eat and drink, and possibly-" He threw a quick side glance at his partner, but Detective Ridley was still praying with his eyes closed. "-have him remain in here with you while we ques-"

Detective Ridley quit praying.

"What?" His eyes snapped open as his head whipped towards his partner. "We can't bring Marsden in here while we question her," Detective Ridley barked.

"It doesn't make a difference if he just sits next to her and keeps his mouth shut," Detective Horrace barked back, and I was rather impressed.

"No," he bit out, shaking his head. "I will not have this case compromised."

"We'll videotape the goddamn thing," Detective Horrace countered, and then looked at me. "Are you okay with us videotaping the interview, Ms. Callows?"

"We are not doing this," Detective Ridley insisted.

I stood up as I smiled at both men. "Well, then, I'll see you boys tomorrow afternoon. Well, unless you're going to go ahead and arrest me. Then I'll see you tomorrow with my lawyer and camera crews." Now, of course, I wouldn't really do that because Theo worked here, and I would never make him a target for hate, but these two buffoons didn't know that.

I stared down at both detectives until Detective Ridley finally caved. "Fine," he snapped. "But this will be videotaped, and Marsden better keep his fucking mouth shut or else we cease the interview, and I *will* throw you in jail, Ms. Callows."

I rolled my eyes.

Childish? Yes.

Warranted? Absolutely.

Both detectives stood up while only Detective Horrace spoke. "We'll be right back with the videotape equipment and Detective Marsden, Ms. Callows."

I gave him my first genuine smile of the night. "Thank you, Detective Horrace. You are the kind of officer that makes *other* officers more tolerable." I said the word 'other' in a tone that was clear to everyone in the room that I was referring to Detective Ridley. I sat back down as I laughed quietly at the sour look on Detective Ridley's face and the beaten look on Detective Horrace's.

It wasn't but a few minutes later that Theo was walking through the interrogation room door, and just like in every romance novel or romantic movie, everything inside me settled and almost everything else was right with the world again. It didn't hurt that he was carrying a bottled water, a bag of chips, and a couple of granola bars.

He walked over until he was standing over me, and the man had the sexiest smirk dancing across his lips. "I wasn't sure what to get you, but I heard you were hungry?"

My smile showed all my teeth. "What else did you hear?"

Theo shook his head as he let out a small laugh. "I also heard that you're a goddamn pain in the ass."

Before I could respond, the door opened, and Detectives Horrace and Ridley were walking in, carrying the videotape equipment.

As soon as Detective Ridley saw Theo, he said, "I mean it, Marsden. *Not one fucking word.*" I laughed as Theo flipped him the middle finger.

Yeah, everything was right in my world again.

CHAPTER 34
No. Fucking. Way.

Theo ~

During Callie's interview, she had received a phone call from her interim boss, leaving her a voicemail that told her to take the next couple of days off. I had a feeling that the only reason Callie hadn't argued was because, by the time that she'd been done with her interview, it had been almost midnight. She had probably been too tired to argue about going back to work.

After she'd been questioned, we had decided to come back to her place because I'd wanted her to feel comfortable after everything that she'd gone through. It had also been fucking hell having to sit by quietly as she recounted how Cody had scared and chased her. She'd held her own against Carmen, but I didn't want to think about what could have happened to her had she been cornered by both of them.

So far, with the preliminary interviews out of the way, it looked like Cody hadn't been involved in Margot's murder at all. He'd just wanted the videos that she had of him and Carmen because he hadn't wanted them found, making him a suspect in her murder. He'd kept claiming that he was never going to hurt Callie, but he had scared her and that was enough for me to want to beat him an inch within his life.

Carmen had unwittingly confessed when she'd started ranting and raving about pressing charges against Callie for assault. She'd been so incensed as she rattled off all the reasons to arrest Callie that she hadn't paid any attention to what she'd been saying and had told everyone in the interrogation room how she had no choice in confronting Callie. There was no way that she could let Callie get away with knowing that she'd been the one who had killed Margot. Now, the only reason I knew that much was because, as it had been me and Darren first on the scene, we'd all had to share the details of our involvement with the arrests.

At the end of the day, all I cared about was that Callie was safe and not getting arrested for assault. By the time that we'd left the precinct, she'd agreed to be more cooperative and promised to testify should Carmen's case go to trial. I still had some serious issues with Cody being free, but Callie had assured me that Cody would be fired immediately once the company found out about him having sex with Carmen on company time and property. Not to mention, there was no way that Melko would want to have a person in their employ who had ties to a murderer.

I hadn't said anything last night, but even if Cody wasn't going to be working at Melko anymore, there was no way that I was going to leave Callie on her own. Last night's dose of reality had been too damaging for me to let her continue to live alone.

No. Fucking. Way.

Not after a scare like that.

I turned my head, and the first thing that caught my eye was the slender curve of Callie's neck. Not wanting to fight with her hair, she had thrown it up in a bun last night before we'd gotten into the shower, so it was still up, exposing that soft, sweet, smooth slant of her neck.

I rolled over until I was big spooning Callie's little spoon, and with my arm thrown over her waist, I started placing soft kisses all over the back of her neck. I told myself that if she didn't wake up after a few strategically placed kisses, then I'd just get out of bed and go start on breakfast, but I was pretty sure that I was lying to myself. Callie had been so exhausted when we'd gotten home last night that one quick shower later, she'd been asleep as soon as her head had hit the pillow. Her adrenaline crash had hit her hard, and as much as I'd wanted to celebrate with the fact that she was okay, and that I hadn't lost her to a couple of psychopaths, I had let her sleep.

However, this morning was a different story.

The second that her limbs started stretching, and she was eliciting little moans, I slid the hand that had been warming her stomach downward until I breached the elastic of her pretty, lacey, light green panties.

"Mmmm, Theo…"

I nipped the shell of her ear. "Were you expecting someone else?"

My heart started hammering at the sincerity of what she said next. "I don't want anyone else." She clamped her hand around my wrist, then pushed her hips out, meeting my fingers halfway. "I don't think it'll be possible for me to ever want anyone else. Mmmm…" Her breath hitched as she added, "Not with how much I love you."

Now, not much could get a guy to pull his fingers out of his woman's pussy-the kids running into the room, a knock at the front door, cops shining a flashlight into your window-but hearing her declaration of love in person and not over the phone in a panic…well, you know it's real and special. So, unfortunately for my dick, that declaration of love warranted me having to remove my fingers from her body, so that she could look at my face while she told me that she loved me.

I pulled my hand out of her panties, and I loved how she immediately started protesting. "Noooo-oh, hey, what are you doing?"

Chuckling, I rolled her over until I was able to settle my body over hers comfortably. When I had the full attention of her soft, content, lazy, green gaze, I said, "You don't get to do that, Callie."

She seemed momentarily dazed just looking up at me, and I realized why when she completely ignored what I'd said and replied with, "You are so beautiful that it hurts my eyes sometimes."

I leaned down, then kissed the curve of her jaw. "Baby, you're too much," I whispered against her skin.

"How so?" she asked while she arched her neck, trying to give me more access to her neck.

I pulled back, so that I could look into her face again. "The first time you tell me you love me, it's over the phone while you're in danger." Her face flushed, and I knew that she was feeling embarrassed or nervous. This was big. "The second time you say it, it's with my fingers buried in your pussy." Callie moaned, and my dick was getting harder by the second. "Now, while both times mean the world to me, I need you to say it when you're not distracted by fear or lust, baby."

Callie brought her hands up to cradle my face, and as serious as she could be, said, "I love you, Theo. I'm *in* love with you, and I probably have been since I snuck out on you the morning after our first night together."

What was a guy expected to do next once he's been handed everything he's ever wanted?

I smiled down at her. "I'm pretty sure that I fell in love with you when we were outside the restrooms at Benji's, and you asked me if I was real," I chuckled, and then as seriously as I could-because I wanted her to know just how real this was-I said, "I love you, Callie Callows." She smiled up at me. "I love you so fucking much, and there is nothing that I won't do to keep you with me."

Her answer was to hook her thumbs inside the waistband of my boxers, then pushed them down over my ass. Next, she spidered her legs to push them all the way down until I was kicking them off and onto the bed. The second that my underwear were gone, I was already propping myself up higher to give her room to pull off her tank top as I worked her panties down her thighs and over her legs.

As soon as we were both completely naked, I settled back over her body at the exact same time that she spread those soft, creamy, perfect thighs of hers wider to accommodate me. My fingers must have done their job because I was able to slide into her tight warmth in one fluid thrust.

Callie's back arched as her head crashed back into the pillow. "Theo…"

All I could do was stare down at her as she took me inside her body. It was a sight that I knew I'd never get tired of. It was a sight that I wanted to see for the rest of my fucking life. If there was a more stunning sight than Callie being fucked, I'd never seen it before.

There was so much that I was feeling between her walking out on me, us making up, her being in danger, and her professions of love, that I didn't know where to even start expressing everything that I was feeling for her, so I just decided on simple. "I love you, baby."

"Oh, God…" Callie opened her eyes as she looked up at me, her face flushed with heat, and her eyes dilated with lust. "Prove it," she challenged. I smirked down at her because I was more than happy to do just that.

I planted my left hand flat on the bed beside her while I wrapped my other hand around her throat, and making sure to trap her eyes with mine, my gaze never wavered as I started pounding into her, giving her everything that I had.

When she couldn't take it anymore, her eyes slammed shut, and she gave herself over to the tremors wracking her body. "Prove it like that?" I taunted. "Or do you need more convincing?" Of course, I didn't expect or wait for an answer. I just kept pushing through the spasms strangling my cock until Callie was screaming for The Good Lord above.

Once her tremors subsided, I let go of her neck, then hooked her knee around my elbow, so that I could open her up more. I started ramming into her so hard that I could actually feel the bruising against my pelvis. Still, she didn't tell me to stop. In fact, Callie screamed for more, and it wasn't until she was clenching all around me again, that I gave myself up to the fall.

I came so hard that white spots danced behind my eyes, and my breath actually hitched. I didn't stop thrusting inside her until the last drop left my body, and I couldn't hold myself up any longer. I collapsed right on top of her, and then rolled us over, so that she was lying across my chest where she belonged.

Where she would always belong.

I couldn't hear anything over the sounds of our breathing and the thumping of our hearts, and it was perfect. Better yet, when Callie dragged her leg over my groin, and I could feel my cum dripping out of her pussy onto my skin, that's when I realized that nothing could be more perfect than this moment with her.

"I love you, baby," I said again, kissing the top of her head.

"I sure hope so," she retorted. "It's not every day that nine inches of penis comes your way."

We didn't stop laughing for over ten minutes.

CHAPTER 35
Priorities.

Callie ~

Two days later, I was back in my office, and I was surrounded by Jay, Brent, Lucia, and Ryan. Beverly had already gone on her vacation, and that was a good thing because she didn't strike me as the type that would have been able to handle all the tension in the building. Now, while I still didn't really trust Ryan, so far, he was acting decent. Maybe it was just Margot that had brought out the worst in him.

"I just can't believe...I mean..." Ryan stuttered. "I had a feeling that it was Carmen, but holy shit, I never imagined that it was because she'd been screwing Cody."

"No shit," Lucia agreed.

It still all felt surreal. According to Detective Horrace, Carmen was still professing her innocence, but between my testimony, Cody's statement, and the witness statements from Detectives Horrace, Ridley, and Franklin, she didn't stand a very good chance of convincing anyone of the story that she was spinning.

As always, Jeremiah was sitting on my desk as Brent, Lucia, and Ryan took up the chairs surrounding my little discussion table. "I can't believe you went all Jason Statham on her," Jay laughed as he reached over, then rubbed over the small bruise on the corner of my jaw.

I huffed. "I think the only reason she didn't kick my ass was because she was shocked stupid when I went after her. She hadn't been expecting it."

"Carmen and Cody..." Brent muttered, finally joining in on the conversation. He'd come in with everyone else, but up until now, he hadn't said anything. I thought maybe he was just shocked or weirded out.

Jay glanced over at him. "Right? I mean, what the actual fuck?"

Brent shook his head. "I just...I always thought he..." He appeared to really be stumbling with this. "I don't know what I thought," he amended. "I just never saw him with Carmen."

"Oh, God. I can't even imagine what Carmen's poor husband and children are thinking," Lucia added. "I mean, if we can barely wrap our minds around it, I can't imagine what they're going through right now."

I hadn't been close with Carmen, but I did know that she was married and had two sons and a daughter. I wasn't sure of the ages, but I knew that her children were all out of high school, so I supposed that was something. They were all somewhat adults, so maybe they'd be better able to deal with everything. I mean, I wasn't sure how anyone could deal with finding out that, not only was their mother having an affair with a guy half her age, but she was a goddamn murderer to boot. Nonetheless, I hoped for the best for them.

"It's got to be one of the most painful things they'll ever experience," Ryan remarked. "I love my wife very much, and the thought of discovering that she was having an affair, and that she cared about the man enough to *kill* for him? Christ."

I hadn't thought of it that way. He had such a heartbreaking point. I tried to think of how I would feel if Theo ever found himself in love with another woman, so much that he'd risk his entire life for her, and I couldn't even imagine it without feeling an actual pang in my chest. Plus, I wasn't even married to the man. We didn't have any kids together, or a twenty-year history.

Oh, God, her poor husband.

"Do you really think Cody had no idea?" Lucia asked.

I just shrugged a shoulder because I honestly had no idea. "I don't know, Luc. Before all this, I would have said that I could never see Cody as an accomplice to murder. However, before all this, I would have sworn that he'd never have an affair with Carmen, so what the hell do I know?"

Jeremiah reached his arm out, wrapped his hand around the back of my neck, then pulled me forward, kissing the top of my head. "I'm just so glad you're okay, Cee Cee."

My eyes prickled at his sincere affection. Jay was usually so good about being professional at work, and it was sweet that he didn't care what Brent, Lucia, or Ryan thought about our friendship right now. His relief that I was safe took precedence over workplace gossip, and that made me feel special.

I looked up at him as I blinked away the moisture in my eyes. "Thanks, Jay." I smiled. "I'm fine, though. Honest."

He smirked. "I guess it helps to have a cop for a boyfriend."

My smile got bigger. "It doesn't hurt."

Just then, the phone on my desk rang. I saw that it was the front lobby and answered. "Hello, Callie Callows speaking."

Bethany, the front lobby receptionist, said, "Hi, Ms. Callows. I have a Detective Marsden here to speak with you, but I don't see that he has an appointment."

If possible, my smile grew bigger. "It's okay, Bethany. Please send him up." I hung up, and when I looked up, Jeremiah was already smirking.

"More official police business, Cal?"

"Shut up, you," I laughed, then I scanned the room and added, "Uhm, Theo's on his way up if you guys don't mind." That was just politeness for the sake of politeness. I didn't care if they did mind. I realized, rather quickly, that in order to make a relationship with a cop work, we had to make each other a priority; there was no other way around it.

Everyone stood up, then started shuffling out the door with their random 'goodbyes' and 'see you laters', but what surprised me was how Ryan stayed back as all the others filed out. Jeremiah gave me a bit of a confused look, but I gave him a quick nod to let him know that it was okay.

Once everyone was gone, I looked up at Ryan. "Everything okay?"

He looked down at me, and his face was so full of genuine emotion. "I'm just really glad you're okay, Callie," he said. "I know we've never been close, and I know I don't have the best reputation as being a good guy, but I really do like you. I've always thought you were…well, I'm just glad you're okay."

"Thank you, Ryan," I replied, and I found that I really did mean it. Maybe Margot's death was allowing Ryan to be a better version of himself. "And maybe we can work on being closer," I suggested.

"I'd like that," he said, smiling. "I'd actually like to get to know all of you a bit better. Hell, maybe a lot more will change around here with her gone."

Before I could reply, Theo's big frame was taking up the doorway. "Callie."

Ryan smiled down at me, then nodded towards Theo as Theo moved aside to let him pass. Theo's eyes followed him until he was well past the door entrance. It was silly, but a small part of me felt like a giddy fourteen-year-old girl with a crush. I didn't need Theo to be jealous of other men, but it did boost my feminine ego when he was.

Theo shut the door behind him, then jerked his head backwards. "What was that all about?"

I walked up to him, wrapped my arms around his waist, then looked up at his handsome face that was all lined with irritation. "He was just telling me that he's happy I'm okay, and he's hoping to become more of a…team member now that Margot is gone," I said, chuckling.

Theo's lips curved down wryly, "As long as he's looking to be a part of the work team and not on anyone's *personal* team."

"*Anyone's* personal team?" I asked, teasing.

His eyes narrowed. "Fine," he growled. "I mean, *your* personal team. I couldn't care less about anyone else." The giddy fourteen-year-old was in full dork dance mode in the middle of her pink bedroom.

"I see no one but you, Detective Marsden," I informed him, adding a little flirtation to my voice.

Theo's shoulders hunched as he grimaced a bit. "Can we stick to Theo?" he asked. "If these past few weeks are any indication, nothing good comes out of you calling me Detective Marsden."

My arms dropped as I stepped back, laughing at him. He had a point, but I couldn't ignore how adorable he looked with his mind filled with flashbacks of me calling him Detective Marsden.

Once I was able to stop laughing, I asked, "What if we're role playing? Can I call you Detective Marsden, then?"

Theo reached for me, then after wrapping me up in his arms, dropped my ass on top of my desk, so that he was standing between my opened legs. "So, if I'm the detective in this little role-playing exercise, what are you?" he asked with his hands gripping my hips.

I scoffed all offended like. "The hooker looking to get out of a bust. *Duh?* What kind of cop are you that you don't know how this scene plays out?"

Theo threw his head back as he let out the most lyrical, beautiful laugh. He looked back down at me as he answered, "I'm the kind of cop that would never trade street-corner sex for getting out of a bust." He leaned down, then gave me a quick kiss. "I'm also the kind of cop that has a hot-as-fuck girlfriend waiting for him at home and would never look at another woman for sex, either."

"Good answer, Detective Marsden," I said placing a kiss on his chest.

"So, does that mean we're role playing now?" he asked eagerly.

It was my turn to laugh again. "We've barely become a place where we can be happy to work at again, Theo. I'm not looking to get fired for screwing my boyfriend at work, no matter how hot he might be." I winked at him to let him know that I was disappointed, too. "Anyway, what are you doing here?"

"I came to take you to lunch," he answered. "I got some free time and wanted to spend it with you. Are you free?"

Priorities.

"As a matter of fact, I am."

Theo's hands ran up my thighs. "You know we're really not going to eat, right?"

I placed my hands on top of his. "I was counting on it."

EPILOGUE

Callie – (Five Years Later) ~
I felt the bed dip, then a warm, heavy, masculine arm fall across my waist. One eye popped open, and I could see that it was a little past eleven.

That heavy arm pulled me back until my back was flushed against Theo's chest, deliciously naked groin, and legs. "Mmmm, Detective," I mumbled.

Theo's arm tightened around my waist as his breath danced across the back of my neck. "Sorry," he whispered. "I didn't mean to wake you."

I laid my arm over his, then squeezed his wrist. "I'd rather go without sleep than miss out on any time with you, Detective Marsden," I replied sleepily. Five years later, I still liked to tease Theo by calling him Detective Marsden.

"I got a double homicide earlier today, but I've got more than enough energy to slide inside you, Mrs. Marsden. However, I'm not sure that I have the energy to full-on role play," he joked. "But if that's what you want..."

I chuckled as I rolled over in his arms. His left arm was under me, and his right arm was wrapped around my waist as I settled my head underneath his neck. God, life always felt so perfect when we were holding each other like this. "Would we be falling victim to the old-married-couple curse if I said I'm fine just cuddling with you? That sex can wait until the morning?"

Theo's chest rumbled beneath my cheek. "Did Henry tire you out?"

I smiled. "Did you check on him before you came to bed?"

"Yeah, you know I always do."

"Well, if he seems to be sleeping peacefully, it's because he had me running after him all evening."

Theo let out a low chuckle. "So, are you saying it's too soon for another?"

I wanted to ask him if he was crazy, but when the face of our two-year-old son popped into my head, I couldn't help but warm at the thought of another miniature Theo because that's what Henry was. He was an exact replica of Theo. It's a wonder how I'd ever be able to prove that he's mine without

149

blood tests.

Then, when I realized that he'd be three by the time our second child would be born, that was too many years in between for my liking. I didn't have siblings, so if Theo and I were going to have a big family, well, I wanted my children to be close.

I rolled on top of my husband, then straddled his already hard dick. I started to slowly rub myself back and forth over his bulge. "I can stop taking my pills tomorrow if you're serious," I told him as I started peppering his jaw line with kisses.

Theo's entire body tensed underneath me, his hands tightening on my hips. "Are *you* serious?"

I kept kissing him as I answered in between pecks. "Yes, I'm serious. I want to give you as many children as you want with me, Theo."

He groaned. "Baby, don't say that. I'll have you pregnant every ten months if you say shit like that."

I laughed as my heart filled with Theo's love. Luckily, being married to Theo was great for my self-image. He loved, cherished, and desired me so completely that I hadn't broken down at the sight of my first stretch mark. I hadn't cried when I'd bought my first pair of maternity pants. My pregnancy had been a celebration of life, change, and love for the entire nine months, and I had this beautiful man beneath me to thank for it.

I had believed Theo when he'd told me that I'd never looked more beautiful than I'd had with each change of the body that was giving him his child. So, it wouldn't bother me one bit to go a couple of more rounds.

"Since we're not millionaires, why don't we settle on a reasonable number, and then start making it a reality tomorrow?"

"Three," he said without any hesitation.

"Okay," I agreed, now kissing his collarbone, still rubbing my pussy across his dick. "Three it is."

Theo's hands started making their way from my hips to my ass. "Unless they end up being all boys," he amended. "Then we go for four because I want at least one little girl."

I started trailing kisses down his chest and over the planes of his hard, sexy, ripped abs. "At least one little girl," I murmured against his skin.

Suddenly, Theo grabbed my arms, then hauled me back up his body until his hands were tangled in my hair and my face was hovering over his. "I love you, Callie." His hands tightened in my hair, and it almost hurt. "I love you so fucking much, baby."

"Even if you don't get a girl?" I teased.

He shrugged. "I'm okay with loving only one girl for the rest of my life if that's the case, then."

Just like that, I fell in love with Theo Marsden all over again.

The End.

ABOUT THE AUTHOR

M.E. Clayton works full-time and writes as a hobby. She is an avid reader and, with much self-doubt, but more positive feedback and encouragement from her friends and family, she took a chance at writing, and the Seven Deadly Sins Series was born. Writing is a hobby she is now very passionate about. When she's not working, writing, or reading, she is spending time with her family or friends. If you care to learn more, you can read about her by visiting the following:

Smashwords Interview

Bookbub Author Page

Goodreads Author Page

OTHER BOOKS

Duets & Series

The Enemy Duet
The Seven Deadly Sins Series
The Enemy Series
Resurrecting the Enemy (Enemy NG Standalone)
The Enemy Next Generation (1) Series
The Enemy Next Generation (2) Series
Embracing the Enemy (Enemy NG Standalone)
The Buchanan Brothers Series
The How to: Modern-Day Woman's Guide Series
The Heavier…Series
The Holy Trinity Series
The Holy Trinity Duet
The Vatican (Holy Trinity NG Standalone)
The Holy Trinity Next Generation (1) Series
The Holy Trinity Next Generation (2) Series
The Eastwood Series
The Blackstone Prep Academy Duet
The Problem Series
The Pieces Series
The Rýkr Duet
The Order of The Cronus Series
The Canvas Duet
When The Series
Expectations Series
The Carmel Springs Series: The Colters
The Carmel Springs Series: The Campions
The Syndicate Duets
The Sports Quintet Series
The Storm Series
The Weight Series
The Through Duet

Standalones

Unintentional
Purgatory, Inc.
My Big, Huge Mistake
An Unexpected Life
Real Shadows
You Again
Merry Christmas to Me
Dealing with the Devil
The Loudest Love
Kimmy & The World of Dating

The Right Price
Work Benefits
The Reading
Noctis
Unusual Noises
Murder or Margaritas
Tell Me Your Truths
All of My Life
A Different Kind of Hooker
It's Never *Not* Been You

Made in the USA
Columbia, SC
12 December 2024